STONEWALL INN EDITIONS
Keith Kahla, General Editor; Mikel Wadewitz, Associate Editor

CALL ME.

by P-P Hartnett

St. Martin's Press ⚏ New York

An extract from *Call Me* has previously appeared in *Technopagan* (Pulp Faction 1995)

The following extracts appear with permission:
O Superman (for Massenet) by Laurie Anderson. © 1982 Difficult Music. Reprinted with permission of the author.
Useless Man—Minty Leigh Bowery, Richard Torry, Carl Fysh, Ingo Vauk (Candy Records 1995). Lyrics reproduced by kind permission of Nicola Bowery and Candy Records. © 1996
Pink And Fluffy—Poly Styrene Lyrics reproduced by kind permission of Poly Styrene. Flower Aeroplane © 1996
My Daughter's Wedding by Donald Urquhart and Sam Ibrahim (aka Sheila Tequila), which appeared in 1994 as a flyer for the club The Beautiful Bend. Extracts (in the church scene of this book) by kind permission.

Visit Stonewall Inn on the World Wide Web:
http://www.stonewallinn.com

Library of Congress Cataloging-in-Publication Data

Hartnett, P-P
    Call me / P-P Hartnett.—1st Stonewall Inn ed.
       p.   cm.
    ISBN 0-312-18063-2
    I. Title.
PR6058.A697C35   1998
823'.914—dc21   97-42219
                                                CIP

First published in Great Britain by Pulp Books, an imprint of Pulp Faction

First Stonewall Inn Edition: January 1998

10   9   8   7   6   5   4   3   2

Michael Cashmore
1958-1971

WITHOUT
RAY

The barboy had skin still tanned from weeks on a beach all by himself. Ivory toenails, perfect fingernails, prepared for compliments. A handsome, sharply groomed, gym-trained young man who gave off a whiff of 'the game'. Very *Euro Boy*. Security ✪✪ Sex ✪✪✪✪✪ Style ✪✪✪✪.

Village was one of those Soho faggot bars that went to town pretending to be laid-back in a New Age kind of way. Lots of varnished wood, stainless steel and lighting you wouldn't notice. Very Amsterdam. The colour scheme was suited to a multi-ethnic reception class.

I had spent the past two weeks decorating my flat, and was feeling fragile. Painting the walls therapeutic colours, Clearly Pink in the bedroom, bathroom and hall, Sweet Apricot in the living-room and kitchen, had ground me down—even though the paint spread with a lovely thickness. Ray had been there to help the last time.

My hands were dried out, there was Polyfilla under the nails and deep in the cuticles. I was exhausted but knew that every last job had been done and when I returned with fruit from Berwick Street I'd soak in the bath before working on my body. It was a comfort to be wearing clean clothes, even though they were Ray's. I fancied a drink, but when the barboy cocked his ear to my mouth I asked for a peppermint tea. A tea-bag was flung into a stained stainless steel teapot desperately needing an overnight soak in bleach.

It was shortly after four, the place had only just opened for business. The music was on low. Without it, the only sound would have been the swallowing of adam's apples and the creaking of necks as heads swivelled in synchrony, following the progress of anything TBH. Village: an unlikely place to have met a *real* blokish bloke.

An anonymous sexual compulsive in search of a fresh face, a new body—some magical quality to feel complete— fixed his sad eyes on me. In hopeful anticipation, he sat up, leaning slightly forward like a proud little boy on his potty, smiling my way as I fixed on the surely-bad-for-business state of the teaspoon slung alongside my cup. The state of anticipation he was trapped in was exhausting the poor soul. He'd perfected that wanna-suck-you-right-this-minute look with years of practice, it was flashing across his forehead more garishly than the neon of Ginza.

As Madonna finished singing about the mystery of life he removed his glasses gingerly, from one ear at a time, staring hard at me. Gently massaging the sore and reddened hollows at the side of his nose, he began to gobble up every curve in my boil-washed Levi's.

I looked away. I wasn't happy with my reflection in the perfect silver disc, a downward-looking me. The special-offer sticker had left a smudge on the case. The CD failed to fill me with the excitement of vinyl; the cover photo of Morrissey seemed so small and there was no shiny new smell. Replacing my record collection was proving a costly process.

The distraction failed. When I looked up he was still staring, glass in hand, tapping a tired foot along to simple thudding computer pop courtesy of The Pet Shop Boys. I prayed he'd soon be hovering up and down Old Compton Street, in and out of pubs and bookshops, stumbling on his way to the attractions of toilets, car parks, cemeteries, cellars, saunas and places of wild natural beauty all in the name of a bit of fun; seeking the mirage of an orgasm.

If he had a job I'm sure there was a pattern to his excessive absenteeism. Fridays: starting the fun early. Mondays: recovering, home alone in Wembley Park or Stockwell feeling ugly, disgusting and unlovable. A headache after so much amyl and the bother of Canesten applications to that lengthy foreskin rubbed raw. The boot-licking, piss-drinking, finger-frigging, tit-tweaking, love-biting, arse-licking, shit-stabbing, mother-fucking, spunk-loving, ball-busting, cock-sucking, fist-fucking, lip-smacking, thirst-quenching, cool-living, ever-giving useless man.

I could have been wrong about him. Could have been wrong about the barboy on the beach all by himself and the occasional vocational calling of his colleagues—I tend to think the worst of people. I'm full of simpleton assumptions, that's just the way the good Lord made me. Often cruel, cold and lacking in humanity. ("Sneery, superior gay men are probably my least favourite type," a features editor once exhaled at me over a light-box, "even if they are really very nice people underneath.") Maybe he was just killing time, awaiting the approaching hour of his second Twelve Step meeting of the day.

A delivery of free papers created a little movement in the place. To avoid further eye contact I made for them, then moved into an alcove beyond his line of vision. *The Pink Paper, Capital Gay, Boyz* and something I hadn't seen before called *Link Up* kept my eyes busy as the peppermint tea cooled.

Avoiding the obituaries in *Capital Gay*, I made for the back to have my usual laugh at the small ads. Week after week so many people offered themselves up for grabs with their unique selling points. All human life was there, held in those pages, trying to shrug off the stigma of inadequacy and failure. The straw-grabbing opportunities had always held an odd sort of fascination for me. Ever since flicking through my elder sister's copy of *Time Out* at the age of thirteen I'd been struck by the touches of poignancy, humour and revealing hints at life's drama. Week by week those puzzle pieces filled my teenage head with images and mystery that went on to direct and, in a way, destroy my life.

The abbreviations, once obscure, had become almost universally accepted, as if the vernacular had been absorbed through osmosis. Once contact ads were the exclusive domain of the sexual fringe, the suicidal and homicidal, but times had changed. Now, people who would never have dreamed of responding to ads did so regularly. Everyone has read them at some time or other.

Videos, massage, coffee...in Camden Town. Young, slim, smooth, professional? Write today. Simon. Box 79.79

Amputee? Couple seek amputee friends. Nothing heavy. You probably wouldn't normally reply to ads. How about now? ALA. Box 81.53

Double bed has only one partner, 35 yo, hairy chested, fit. Into lycra, jocks, pillow fights and more. Shirtless photo helps. No fats, fems or Maria Callas fans. Box 73.49

Mud-soaked footballer seeks fit, slim, straight-acting guys up to 30 to score with. Do you secretly enjoy getting muddy in football shorts? Playing on swamp-like pitches essential. Non-scene preferred. London only. Box 87.58

RUA Big Boy? Me, gorgeous looks, smooth muscular body, 25. You: WE, active. Size guarantees reply. Box 83.48

American Serviceman, stationed over here. Do you want a discreet friend (30s) on South Coast? (Non smoker. Black/white.) Photo. Box 78.41

Millionaire wanted, 50+, by Dale. (Tall, passive, 19 yo.) Straightlooking + acting. GSOH, loving, loyal and gorgeous for eternal 1-1. Box 83.55

Formal reprimand available from youngish authority figure. Appropriate dress: smart business suit, tie, white shirt. Inexperienced welcome. Discretion assured. ALAWP. Norwich. Box 80.90

CALL ME

5

Until that moment I'd never thought of answering a personal ad, never mind placing one. Maybe it was because the week's selection was so dull that I was almost prompted to say aloud: *I could do better than that!* This set me thinking. It would be intriguing to see the replies, what people said and how they said it. I was curious to see the stationery, the photographs, the handwriting...the spelling even. I wanted to see their fantasies. I wasn't searching for love—I'd stopped being boyfriend-orientated with a jolt three years back. Definitely free from that shackle of hope. I was in the mood for some good, dirty, voyeuristic fun. That's all.

Although familiar with the ads, I'd never looked into the mechanics of it all. I hadn't realised it was so cheap to advertise; just three pounds for a box number open for a month, and up to twenty words, every word thereafter costing fifty pence. The arrangement was more or less the same in *The Pink Paper* and *Link Up*. *Boyz* was way ahead of the rest on categorisation: 'One to One, Pen Pals, Professional Men, Boots and Braces, Locker Room, Leather, Firm Hand, DIY' and several other sections to sadden many a mother. At that time of instability in my life it was free to advertise in *Boyz*, maximum thirty words. People responding to bait laid paid one pound fifty to reply to a single ad, or five pounds for four. Scanning the pages, absorbing the ads in a new way, the ball began to roll.

Gay prisoner, good looking, straight-acting, seeks contacts. It's a lonely life, I need cheering up. Any age will do. Curious? Get writing! Photo please. ALA with SAE. Box PP2006

Group fun your scene? Sunday afternoons come alive just north of M25! (20 mins Kings Cross.) Photo gets reply. Box DIY3801

Pretty boy, 18+, unwashed in dirty underpants, sought by attractive uncle, 40. Raunchy safe fun, poppers, toys, videos. Expenses. ALAWP. Box SP351

Jewish Y-fronts enthusiast WLTM discreet non scene young guy (18-35) wearing white Y-fronts. ALA. London/Anywhere. Uncut welcome! Box LR3139

Scottish guy, new to London and lonely, looking for cool mate to hang out with, club with. Also: concerts, museums, discovering London's parks. Friendship first. Box 003739

Steve. Horny blond boy, 20, seeks beautiful sexy lads in frocks for divine London romance. Photo? Box 003783

Nappies? Plastic pants? Sounds exciting? 28 years old. Box PP 5041

Rubber Alien. Completely concealed inside heavy-duty black frogman's suit and full head mask seeks fellow aliens into similar gear to explore magic of total coverage. Bournemouth/Anywhere. Box NS3096

Distracted by the arrival of a gang of fellow disco sodomites making a Big Entrance replete with tasteful tattoos, jolly piercings and jism-spattered combats (dressing up as men but totally Nelly in that khaki drag), screaming their blissed-out tits off and almost losing their gum in the process (a little bit Dean, a little bit Cruise), boys who measure their pleasure in beats per minute but still share their ol' mum's taste in music, boys with heads for business and bods for sin, (stripping off their D&G an' Arsenal away strips at the drop of a clapper-board), boys who just wanna have fun fun fun—goatee beards and sheep mentality—nothing like a little bit of empty-headed hedonism, eh?...but, oh...shouldn't queerbash the sweethearts or plagiarise the odd fag hack with a big nose who knows...When my eyes went back to the page before me, I focussed on a grouping of 0898+ titles in the XXX rated **American Style** phone sex section howling in chorus just to the left of a selection in lavish italics entitled **Specials:** *Intercity Sex, Toilet Trio, Hole Sucking Slave, Hung Like A Donkey,* just to the right of a block boasting **Active:** *Building Site Erections, Young And Easy, Sauna Room Sex, Shoot Over My Face,* just above a collection teasing with **Hot Sex Only:** *Skin-Tight Jeans, Prxxks On Parade, Inflatory Bum Stretcher,* and just below the whispered **Non-Scene South:** *City Cottage Cruising, Don't Tell My Wife, Cross Dress And Confess.* Alongside each title sat a six digit sex code number in neat double sets of three.

The grouping of titles that really caught my eye came under **Lycra:** *Sportswear, Bulging Pants/Bulging Weapon, Boys On Bikes, Thick Muscular Legs/Thick Muscled Meat.* I'd only bought my mountain bike a few weeks before this, so *Boys On Bikes* had a certain appeal. Sure, the titles were real dial-a-cliché but better designed to provoke a reaction than the contact ads. My eyes scanned, intent.

ACCESS THE GAY CODE MENU

No Intros—Just Horny Action!
Lines Open 24 Hours A Day
7 Days A Week
NEW FAST EASY FUN
THE FILTHIEST SLEAZIEST SEX
STORIES
——UNZIP AND DIAL——
TOTAL FANTASY
HOT SECS!
0898 456 ***
GUYS WHO LOVE TO SUCK
(Graphic descriptions of
mind-blowing blow jobs!)
0898 456 ***
SUBMISSION + DOMINATION
(HEAR SLAVES BEING TIED UP
AND USED FOR
BIZARRE CARNAL PLEASURES)
0898 316 ***
CALL THE VOYEUR
0898 316 ***
RUGBY PLAYERS HANDLE BALL
0898 316 ***
FILTH AND FETISH
0898 767 ***
PICK-A-PUNISHMENT
0898 767 ***
PICK-A-PACKET
0898 767 ***
TOTAL DEGRADATION
DIAL NOW—TOTAL
FANTASY—COME ON!
0898 767 ***
BLACK
0898 767 ***
GREEK
0898 767 ***
DILDO

0898 767 ***
PVC
0898 767 ***
MEAN AND ANGRY
0898 767 ***
ENDLESS ERECTION
GO ON...DROP 'EM AND DIAL!
0898 556 ***
BLACK CABBIE (10" of hard
black muscle.)
0898 556 ***
BUS DRIVER
(Rear Action)

GO ON...GET OFF OVER THE
PHONE! SURRENDER TO DESIRE!
DIAL NOW!
RELIEF IS IN YOUR HANDS!
"American Style" Multi-Choice
Numbers For Touch-Tone Phones
GO ON...DROP 'EM AND DIAL!
THAT'S AN ORDER!
DIAL 0898 PLUS YOUR CHOSEN
SEX CODE AND LET YOUR
FINGERS DO THE WORKING
LINES FOR INFORMATION
LINES FOR CONFESSIONS
LINES FOR DATING
Telephone Dating that takes
you even deeper Who knows
who you could meet? Get some
interactive action—Dial now!
FIND A FRIEND, MAKE A DATE

Calls charged at 39p per minute cheap rate,
49p per minute at other times.
Remember, when meeting a date:
Be safe and sensible.
Meet in a public place.
Tell a friend.

OVER 18s ONLY.

CALL ME

8

Bouncing heavily on the springboard of fantasy, I thought I'd paint a horny picture to turn them on out there. I decided it should be very visual, thirty dirty words reading more like a phone-sex line description than a personal ad. With just a little browsing through the queer image bank I was ready. From the moment my ball point touched the paper serviette I'd entered the arena. Lopping four years off my age and pouring myself into a pair of cycle shorts I didn't possess, I wrote the ad all in one go.

> **Bike Boy:** delicious derrière under shiny black skin-tight cycle shorts. (Long smooth muscular legs. 22/Slim/Safe/WE/Wicked smile.) Horny devil seeking adventure. Any time/Any place/ Anywhere. Genuine.

Genuine my arse. Cycle shorts, lycra: how naff. And how fabulous. The ideal hook for provincial schoolboys and hideous queens.

Swallowing my tea in gulps, I loaded my pannier with a shove. My admirer gulped down a rear view. Gay love is not blind. He would have recoiled at the sight of a concave chest, double chin or absence of copious bulge in the dong department. He wanted prime, pumped, waxed, tanned, moisturised boy-flesh. A nice bit of muscle drag. No short-dicked man. I gave him a wink and a winning smile as I left, hoping it would make his day, fuel a noisy wank or two.

When I got back to the gloss-stinking flat, I checked the wording, filled in the word-space boxes in capital letters as requested, ticked the 'No Strings' box and tucked it in an envelope with a first-class stamp.

Then I rolled the dustsheets away and removed any lingering drips of pink and apricot paint with a dab of turps on my newly retired *Nobody Knows I'm A Lesbian* teeshirt. I like things tidy: balanced chequebooks, punctuality, polished shoes lined up under the bed, shoelaces exactly even. Well-maintained graveyards.

Up till then I'd led the average life of the average unhealthy young man. With my camera I froze people, proclaimed ownership over their images, put words into their mouths then sold them to tacky fashion and music magazines. I'd done well for myself, made quite a name for myself. I didn't care. I was bored.

Work had become uninspiring and undemanding but not financially unrewarding. Fashion and music in the giddy, topsy-turvy, pervy Nineties: always changing, always moving. Fashions adopted then discarded. Knowledge gained then outdated. Ideas created only to be burned up. At twenty six, the curvaceous rises and falls of the record sales charts no longer gripped me. I no longer wanted my place in that world of mass hypnotism with ever faster pulsing cycles of nostalgia, buzzwords and panty-dampening boy bands with unbroken voices in leather chaps and nipple rings. I didn't even find Vivienne Westwood funny any more.

I had some money in the bank, not a lot, but enough to glide by for a while, so I decided to pack my cameras and portfolio away and glide on by—just for a while. Having at long last got the flat into order was my only accomplishment in months. I'd finally boxed away Ray's bits and pieces; what had once been his flat, then ours, was now all mine. My few friendships were all worn down and Ray's friends had stopped checking in to see if I was okay. Nobody had a clue about the mood percolating in my seventh floor flat.

It was as if whole sides of myself were shutting down. Taking life five times slower than the national average, I wasn't up to much except sleeping. I am a man who has slept years of daylight. The invitations and press passes piled up, then dried up. That's what happens if you fail to RSVP. Sometimes, for light relief, I'd make popcorn, have a wank or shop at Sainsbury's for exotic items never sampled before. I was at that stage in my life where a quick read of *How To Be A Happy Homosexual* might have proved inspirational. I felt I had two options, emigration or suicide.

Waking later and later each day a sadder self arose to make the tea. Eventually I'd manage to be up around eleven, having rarely slept well. Mornings were worst.

It happened the day after I'd shampooed the carpets in the hope of turning over a new leaf. The overstuffed envelope didn't fit the letter-box but my plodding, polyester postman wasn't going to ring, wait and deal with someone, especially someone like me. He had a round to get done, letter-boxes to violate. After noisy pushing and shoving it finally landed like an abandoned origami effort. The letter-box let in a chill, smelly breeze which swept into the bathroom, directly opposite the front door.

The thin, brown stationery tore easily and Bike Boy replies cascaded to the bathroom floor. As with exam results and private letters I sat naked, on the toilet, to read sackfuls of desire, a whole pot pourri of emotions, stamps licked by the psychologically wounded, the emotionally bankrupt and *fun seeker*s. I was to become a receptacle for first impressions to all sorts making life-directing bungee jumps.

Counting the small envelopes contained within, thirty eight, I felt quite a thrill. I classified the envelopes before opening, stacking the coloured envelopes in one pile, the cheap little crushed envelopes in another, leaving the fine quality Queen's Velvet sort of stuff to one side. As I read, I sorted the letters into *Yes*, *No* and *Maybe* piles around my feet. I felt like an impartial party sent to observe. Bike Boy had hit the crackpot jackpot.

A pre-war Remington had typed the first man's desires. The capitals jumped into the course above on all three sheets of expensive cream coloured Conqueror paper. A first class stamped addressed envelope was optimistically enclosed. Also enclosed was a photograph, taken against a white wall reflecting noon sunlight. His face wore an expression of determination to look good on photographic paper but the overhead light cast shadows which didn't do any favours. His plain body was dressed sensibly.

The sample of pubic hair attached to the left of his address, brown to ginger, was crudely attached with a strip of sellotape bearing one clear fingerprint.

—, —— ——,
Market Bosworth,
Nuneaton,
Warwickshire
Tel: 01455———

Hi, handsome Bike Boy—my name's Michael and as you can see I live in Market Bosworth near Leicester. I see from your ad in BOYZ that you're "Any place/Anywhere", so I hope this letter isn't a complete waste of time.
Isn't it difficult to know what to write: too tame and one can seem boring, too "exciting" and one can seem a pervert. I'm neither by the way. A little about me now. I'm 39—young looking with blue eyes and brown hair. Reasonably handsome, 5`9``, smooth-skinned. I'm well travelled, quite well educated, have a solid job, own house, car etc. (dull, eh!).
I have a large number of interests from wine to local history, from trying to learn Dutch to fell walking. It was the fell walking which triggered my interest in your ad. I don't go mountain biking but I know the Lake District, Pennines and Scotland very well and am out walking at least once a week.
I don't have a partner, am non-scene and definitely non-camp. I've plenty of holiday left this year, and I fancy taking the station wagon up to Scotland to do some walking.
If we clicked, so to speak, maybe you'd like to come with me. I usually just pitch a tent—I like the open air life. I fancy

a few days in Sandwood Bay, a remote sandy bay facing the Atlantic. You can see gannets diving offshore and the sea gets beautifully rough. I love to watch a stormy coast. I don't suppose Scotland is much of an adventure but it beats London any day! (I'm guessing that's where you're from.) Those cycle shorts sound nice and if we did get you up to Market Bosworth I could find quite a few uses for that delicious derrière you advertise so nicely. I haven't rode a bike for years but I daresay I could ride your bum quite well. After leaving the pub we'd go back to the campsite. Your groin would be aching with expectation. In the tent I would slowly take off your clothes under a large duvet that I use. I would gently ease your legs apart and kiss the inside of your leg as I gradually moved closer to your prick.

I suck your balls and lick your groin before taking your prick deep into my mouth. I suck your balls again and let my dribble run down to lubricate your arse which I have been delicately easing with my index finger. I lift up the duvet and put your legs onto my shoulders and move forward to put my tongue into your mouth. As I do so, my 7" tool slips easily into your arse and I move rhythmically to and fro until I come. We cuddle up and fall asleep.

What a fantasy—what an adventure! Actually, it's all perfectly possible. Just get yourself up here and the rest is my treat. Well Bike Boy, you horny devil, I hope to hear from you soon. Do write a frank letter and if you have a phone number let me know that too. Just the thought of my stiff prick sliding into you for the very first time is making me so excited. Please phone—I shall be waiting.

Best wishes
Yours,
Michael

Verdict: Take a chance? My intuition told me this was a sure way to end up in a shallow grave with my head simmering nicely on the stove. *No.*

From Hampstead came jagged writing on a single sheet of grey. Matching envelope. Stapled top left was a black and white mug-shot.

—, —————— ——
Hampstead
0171 433 ——

Hello Stranger!

You sound great. It gives me a hard-on just thinking about those shorts, or what's in them.
Horny devil? Welcome any time!

Best wishes,
Jack Hanley

Verdict: Without the photo Jack would have been a *No*. But he could have been my twin.

Tall, dark, mid to late twenties. Barbour jacket, estate-agent haircut. Serious. A *Maybe*.

A page torn from a school maths exercise book had been folded several times too many, like a note passed under a toilet door. It came in an envelope too large for such an item. An absolute scrawl in green felt-tip.

Saturday
0171 937 ——

Dear Bike Boy, are you serious?
I feel a little awkward replying
to a lonely hearts ad but suppose
that the mystery element is fun.
Slim / smooth / safe / smiling?
Could it be that there are
actually a few of us around?
I'm 16, about 5'8", blue eyes,
blond(ish)...If interested
then give me a ring.
If I'm not in leave a message.
Be discreet or you'll freak my mum!
Hope to hear from you soon.

X
Allan

Verdict: Show me a queer who'd say no to the idea of a sixteen-year-old and I'll show you a liar. *Yes.* (Guardedly.)

Two signatures with the same black ink, slanting in opposite directions, caught my attention at the bottom of a crisp yellow sheet. Nicely word processed, poorly printed.

————.
————— Lane,
Barnstaple,
North Devon

Dear NS 405,

We are replying to your advert in Boyz.
(Apologies for typing but our writing is hard enough to understand ourselves, let alone for someone else try to decipher it.)
We are Matthew and Gareth and have been together seven years and thought what with the general pressures and frustrations of London, we would fare better in Devon and have recently bought a two bedroomed house down here.
We are both interested in entertaining, videos, Country & Western music, ice-skating, computers. How about you? What are your interests, hates etc? Do you live on your own? Where?
We are both versatile when it comes to sex and both enjoy most aspects of it, except S&M and bondage. We can easily accommodate if you fancy some country air, homemade wine and FUN. Drop us a line and send us a photo, we'd love to see you in those cycle shorts.
All the best now. Looking forward to hearing from you.
Sincerely,
Matthew + Gareth.

Verdict: Nice letter. *No.*

I wasn't expecting to receive a questionnaire. Three pages of airmail paper demanding details in a pencil so sharp at the start, blunt by the finish. It came as a shock. It certainly deserved a merit mark for effort.

—————
—————Road
London —
0181 679 ——

Your abject advert has caught the fancy of this experienced, exotic and pierced Master.

Naturally He wishes to have more intimate details about the property, so you are expected to complete and return the questionnaire at once, using the sae enclosed.

Obeying this order serves as an exercise in physical stocktaking and a mental preparation for the slave status your delicious derrière deserves.

As soon as He receives your reply, the Master will make the necessary arrangements for your first encounter. He can travel to your place or He can accommodate you in Norbury. Though very thorough in examining a slave, the Master finds all types and most combinations interesting and attractive. Attitude is most essential, though negotiated limits are respected.

Now fill this in, underlining neatly, where appropriate, then mail using the sae enclosed without delay. Use a pen! Only a Master writes to a slave in pencil as an added discourtesy.

Name:
Address:
Telephone number:
Date of birth:
Blood group:
Height:
Weight:
Build: skinny/slim/lithe/muscular/fat/or...
(Give details.)_____.
Colouring:_____eyes; _____hair; _____nipples;

CALL ME
17

_____glans; _____anal rim.

Penis length: ____`` flaccid;____`` erect.

Penis girth:____`` flaccid; ____`` erect.

Foreskin: cut/short/shortish/longish/long/
very long/excessive.

Foreskin end: bared glans tip/nozzle/rosette/jug lip
overhang.

Foreskin overhang, (if appropriate):
short/medium/long/excessive.

Length of overhang, (if appropriate):____``.

Foreskin, (if appropriate): stays put when retracted/rolls back
when retracted/retracts naturally when erect/stays hooded
when erect.

Preference: naked glans or hooded glans.

Testicles: small/medium/large/extra large.

Heft: heavy hanging/low hanging/level hanging/one ball
lower than the other/tightly drawn up.

Scrotum: naturally smooth/furry wisps of hair/or_____.

Armpits: sparse hairs/thick tufts/thick & long mane/bushy.

Pit hair: downy wisps/wiry straggle/fleecy/silky skeins.

Nipples: large aureoles/miniscule/medium/or _____.

Teats: inverted/upstanding/big bosses/or _____.

Torso: naturally smooth/hairy/shaved/waxed/or_____.

Limbs: naturally smooth/fine hairs/hairy/shaved/waxed/or

_____.

Buns: full/meaty/meagre/tight/loose/or_____.

Crack: naturally smooth/sparse hairs/hairy/or _____.

Pubes: small patch/large pelt/extending from navel/or

_____.

Pubic hair type: cropped down/downy wisps/thick fleece/wiry
bush/wild tangles /silky/or _____.

List your top six specialities, (services unto a Master):

1:

2:

3:

4:

5:

6:

List limitations, (use other side if necessary):
Desire takes many forms:
nudity/restraints/blindfolds/boots/CP/Yellow/verbal
abuse/humiliation/toys/leather/shaving...List your desires
below, (use other side if necessary):

_____

_____

_____

_____

_____

_____ (P.T.O.)

Days available:
Times available:
Travel by private or public transport:

So, you horny devil, fill this out honestly and I'll make sure
you'll smile. A slave offering his delicious derrière knows only
the minimum about his future master. This uncertainty adds
to his predicament, intensifies his bondage. The Master, on
the other hand, expects to know about every private part and
have the most intimate questions answered.
You should enclose photos (if possible) and quote your box
number.
Much will be demanded of you at the first encounter.
Prepare to meet a dominant & exotically pierced Master.

If you fancy a chat about any of this then give me a call.
Eamon

CALL ME

19

Verdict: *No.* No way.

Inside the small plain white envelope there was one hell of an A4. Even before taking it out into the air of my flat, I sensed something nasty coming my way. Much of the large, forcefully written page was smudged.

—, —— Street,
London SW4.

Hello there young friend,
very interested with your "different type" advert But I doubt very much as to whether you will want to reply or meet up with me due to my oldish age Still for the sake of £1.50 and a stamp—I'll take a chance
At time of writing I am 49yrs and 11 days old so to you at 22 that's far too old. But can definitely assure you I'm not yet past it —Neither am I some aging camp queen like a lot of this age I'm very Masculine—straight looks and Ways
Also, 6`—slim—11 stone—active—NON Good Looking At this age what can you expect? I am very genuine + sincere unlike a great majority today—Most cant even spell the words—I'm very Experienced—so not a 5 min time waster
Varied Interests—one of these being Shorts—Especially your style (Skin Tight) That helps show off a guy at his best + hottest—more so if he's got plenty to display (Front + Rear) inside them—But keen on all styles of hot shorts—Looking forward to the summer, hope! To see them all on show again in the parks etc etc
I'll keep this brief as I said earlier Doubt very much if you will have any further interest in me—I'm fairly certain you will be getting a big response with other younger replies But if you should want to make contact then lets know all about you—and if you do have a pix in your gear Like to see it —Will be returned, promise. Cheers for now.
John Pumphrey

PS Please do not just turn up at my door.

Verdict: Obvious.

Three small thin sheets of light blue paper, cheap as you can get. Sloppy, soppy twelve-year-old girl's writing in blue felt tip with some words scribbled out here and there.

—, —— House,
Deptford.
0181 692 ——

Hi,
I have just seen your add in Boyz. I am 21 dark brown hair and eyes 5`9`` in hight 40`` chest 32`` W like bikes but have NOt got a good one. I like XXXXX wight training runing BOXing SWiMMing cars clubs pubs and More do you like cars?
Sorry I can Not send you my PHoto this time because I have just getting to modlling and my XXXXXX agenky has my Photos. I can NOt tell you that I can LOVE you we have to see one anthere I am looking for the Man of My dreams it's not Manly to say so I no.
Peple saye that I Love My Self but I do Not I am just Careful I do not slep around NO way I have Lots of friend good friends but not Speshell to be with one to one and mine.
When I go out clubbing peple Chat Me up all the time but I NO they only Whents one Night Stands If you XXXX like what I have written write back.
From a friend
Costas

PS Can you send me a Photo before meeting if you have one?

PPS I wear glasses......Italian designer frames!

CALL ME

21

Verdict: Maybe. Maybe once allocated a statement of Special Educational Needs. A phone call wouldn't hurt.

The first candidate to submit on headed notepaper. Smart, very crisp. Expensive. The signature, in blue italics, contrasted with the formal and very faint type. There was a very strong public school stink to it all. Stamped addressed envelope enclosed, first class.

—, ———— Road,
South Kensington.
Tel: 0171 838 ——

Dear Delicious,
I'm a young City professional and regarded by some as good looking. Being trussed up in three piece pinstripe suits five days of the week, your ad really turned me on!
Phone/write and we will get together.

Good luck,
Colin.

PS Please excuse the typed letter, I don't mean to be insincere.

Verdict: Sorry Colin, uh uh.

A postcard. A three-colour computer graphic produced by someone in Stockholm. One of the give-away kind found in so many of the bars. Stylish capitals, slanting to the right, looked sane.

To the owner of the delicious derrière...

Darling...We must meet! You sound interesting. I never find writing letters, or cards, convincing. Please phone me instead.
I can be reached on 0181 691 ——. (Brockley).
I'm considered attractive by some, interesting by others etc. I'd prefer to spend an afternoon chatting + perhaps drawing. I shall entertain you with food + wine + we can decide if we want to know each other. What do you say?

Best wishes
Charles

Verdict: Drawing? This meant going to the man's home. Perhaps he'd ply me with drink, suffocate me while sleeping, dismember me in some sort of ritual to be finished with as quickly as possible once he'd had his way with my corpse, flushing my flesh down the toilet and into the sewers in sushi-style six-inch strips.

Yes, yes please.

Lurking inside a light green envelope, a black and white picture documenting a goofy, failed physique model in white ankle socks, Y-fronts, string vest and all-American style baseball jacket. Camp: James Dean has a lot to answer for. A backdrop of venetian blinds—very *American Gigolo*. A potted fern to one side added a certain tropical touch.

The handwriting was all over the place, a graphologist's dream sample.

PHONE: 01323 --- ---

Dear Box NS405...or can I call you Box?

Hi, My name is Derrick. I've just read your advert and my prick has never got so stiff so quickly. I often walk along the seafront in Hastings, Eastbourne and Brighton, watching young sports guys. The cyclists stop, get off their bikes and the sexy black shorts show clearly the outline of rigid cock. Then they turn around, I catch a glimpse of well-formed buns, nice deep crack up it. Sadly I have never met one who is gay, but I have been tempted, very tempted, to touch.

I'd love to get you cycling around a bit until you are hot, then get you into a private room (a beach hut would be nice) and run my soft hands all over your body. I would spend a while exploring the warmth of your skin thru that shiny black, then we would peel our clothes off. My prick would spring to life and my shaven balls and ass would be ready for anything. As I peel your shorts etc off my tongue would taste the fresh hot sweat between your legs and between your cheeks etc etc etc.

Anyway, here's a photo of me. I'm 5' 10", not camp. and have my own transport. If this letter is of interest, phone 01323 - -- --- any Tuesday 8-8.30pm. This is a public callbox. (Nosey flatmate and fear of crank calls!)

I hope I am suitable for your fantasies — Derrick

PS Forgive my trashy writing.

Verdict: I could imagine him jerking off over a sweet-smelling new magazine, fascinated by the shadows that nestle under hamstrings and ribs, little brown bottle shoved up one nostril. *No.*

A real money feel to the stationery from Anthony (Tony to his friends.) Smart, crisp, off-white. Ten out of ten writing. Two enclosures:

1) A snapshot taken in Seville showing an okay to good-looking blond, perhaps just over the worst of flu.

2) A minty flavoured *Mates* condom.

—, ——————— Mews,
Kensal Green.

Hi,

My name is Anthony Beckett, (Tony to my friends). I'm twenty five and as you can see from the photo I'm blond, blue eyed. It's no big deal but I've never answered a personal ad before, I guess one's never really caught my attention—until now that is. (It's a bit of a shock having to enclose a cheque for £1.50p!) You see, I really get turned on by bike-gear!—Really! Especially those very shiny, black skin-tight lycra shorts your ad teased with so well. Kinda feel like a dirty old man writing all this but, what the hell...

Me—well, I don't ride bikes that often. My passion is canoeing. I do it every other day. I live near a canal and so after work me and my single kayak go onto the canal for an hour or so to clear my head.

I really like those narrow *Bike* jockstraps too. There's a shop in Covent Garden which I go into on the weekend for my weekly "fix". The photo enclosed was taken in Spain recently. I would be grateful if you could return it with your reply. Anyway, I look forward to hearing from you.

Cheers,
Tony

Verdict: On the one hand he sounded a bit naff, on the other there was this image of him canoeing along in the shadow of the Harrow Road which appealed to the romantic in me. A *Maybe*.

Black ink on top of the range beige aroused the whore in me. First class stamped addressed envelope plus a ten-unit phone card enclosed.

—————.
—, ————— Avenue,
South Harrow
0181 422 ——

Dear Bike Boy,

Your advertisement in <u>Boyz</u> has certainly struck a chord in this committed mountain bikist. Although 52 I'm passionate for everything to do with them and believe your form of dress to be the only civilised one!
Do come and see me as soon as poss'. Tel: 0181 422 ——. (As above.)
I've lots of other interests too: music, photography, videos etc. I commute to London daily on my Muddy Fox Monarch or my Saracen, (improved!). I travel to and from Hong Kong a lot on business.
I've been thinking about you ever since a friend rang, informing me of the ad. It's a fabulous advertisement, you make yourself sound perfect.
I hope to hear from you soon, you delicious horny devil!

Greetings,
Phu Mok

PS Garden is big.

Verdict: Yes. I fancied seeing the garden.

The glossy colour photograph might have been the Bike Boy I'd imagined when writing the ad. A Stephen from Richmond, standing alongside his Saracen in full gear, displaying thick muscled legs and small hips. Though suffering from an unfortunate hairdo, perhaps betraying a leaning towards heavy metal, he managed a smile, bottom lip glistening in the sun. Two silver chains in a tangle around his neck. Quite a cock, judging by the shiny contours of his cycle shorts. Untidy writing on paper which bore the imprint of a previous, longer letter. Enclosed, a second class envelope.

—B, ———— Avenue,
Richmond.
0181 940 ——

Dear Bike Boy,

I am writing to you because of our similar interests.
I am also into skin shorts, lycra, smooth muscular legs, horny action.
I am quite a keen cyclist as well!
I train a lot when weather permits so I am reasonably fit.
I am 23 years, 5`11``, slim built.
It would be nice if you replied, you can phone me in the evenings and I enclose an SAE.
I hope to hear from you soon, one way or another.

(Sorry about the writing.)
Stephen.

PS Photo was taken one year ago. My hair's a lot shorter now.

Verdict: Yes. A safe enough start, I thought. He turned out to be the first person I called.

Oh, there were more; page after page, life after life. Letters scented with risk and the rawness of possibility. Invariably these absolute strangers wanted to do those four-lettered verbs: lick, suck, bite, fuck, wank, chew, kiss and—in the case of Charles from Brockley—*draw* Bike Boy. I decided to deal with a few, do some phone tests—maybe meet one or two. The cheap little cartoon gay slag/Adonis I'd invented had become the object of much frenzied nocturnal contemplation.

I could picture them busy behind piles of stationery, with chequebooks and postal orders at the ready. Folding replies neatly, tucking snapshots in carefully. Paper clipping, stapling, moistening stamps, pressing down, licking envelopes, sealing themselves in.

Ages ranged from the sixteen-year-old schoolboy (was that to be believed?) to a fifty-six-year-old barrister's clerk recovering from a heart by-pass op'. A medical student from SE17, leaning back against a radiator—jeans around his ankles—had a particularly nasty spot of ringworm, guess where. A solicitor from Parsons Green sent three used, cellophane-wrapped tissues for me to sniff.

All kinds of names for all kinds of games. Photos of men in rubber, leather, baths, showers, not forgetting Anthony Beckett in Seville. A newsagent from Birmingham, an acupuncturist over in Hammersmith, a bored school teacher in Nepal, a curly-haired hypnotist and an Anglican priest. Holy cock. All felt like pawns for me to control as I wished.

I thought graphology was a pile of shite until the fan mail started. The slant, slope, pressure, spacing, choice of pen—all gave an impression. Even the final signature to a word-processed piece held a message as it diminished into threadlike strokes or pierced the page with fierce triangular loops and stabbing "i" dots.

Few were genuine friendship seekers, but then the ad *was* of the raunchy variety. I neither liked nor disliked these needy characters, all after a spot of reasonably safe sex at little expense. What remote feeling I did have might be likened to the dispassion with which non-animal lovers view cats and dogs.

Tearing the corners off the stamped-addressed envelopes, I soaked them in a small bowl of warm water. With a dab of Pritt Stick, they could be recycled.

I'd never had a problem with my Yamaha. I kept it dry, cool and dust free, cleaning the exterior with a soft cloth. It had never been jolted or dropped. I took the greatest of care when plugging cords into the rear panel jacks, as excessive force can damage the terminals.

I knew it was going to rain, I could feel it in the air, cumulonimbus clouds approaching eastwards.

My Yamaha looked so black against the fresh whiteness of the balcony door, venetian blinds angled just so to protect it from the early morning sun. All numbers and symbols on the buttons of the VOICE/STYLE group had faded away from wear long ago, its only imperfection. The stereo headphones were always plugged in; I'd only used the internal speaker system once and I didn't like it. The internal circuitry featured a maximum polyphony of twenty eight notes which could be played simultaneously, with extra notes when the automatic accompaniment, split, or duel voice features were used. I'd never used more than ten notes in any of my home recordings.

The PSR 300 had touch response—that is, the volume of the sound could to a certain degree be controlled by how hard you played the keys. I preferred sliding the master volume control right up to a position which would win over the Goswell Road. That day I didn't slide the volume up too high. I wanted to hear the rain when it fell. Even with the headphones on I could hear background sound like white noise. I hoped for thunder.

When I pressed the SUSTAIN button, the indicator lit up welcomingly. I selected the fretless bass sound, then improvised on the lower end of the keyboard. Sounds decayed gradually as my fingers lifted from the keys. I liked the way the notes hummed and slurred. The SUSTAIN effect could not be applied to accompaniment or rhythm, which was a shame. I always imagined the drums treated. Unfortunately the SUSTAIN effect didn't sound as deep as usual when it was used during accompaniment.

When I heard thunder I opened the door, emptying out paid-for heat to smell rain on cold wet concrete. Pulse slow, I stood steady and cold against the wind, in awe of the day. My hanging arms, limp and heavy, conducted a low dull tune in my head. A cigarette tossed from the balcony would have have gone out before reaching the ground.

I like the rain in cities, angled in headlights, backlit by advertising and silly windows, raindrops like long silver needles. I saw a woman running for the number 4 bus, handbag on head, left hand holding her wet skirt away from her body so it wouldn't cling. The bus made a rare exception, pulling up fifteen yards or so from the stop and I smiled and shivered as she looked for loose change.

When it rains I like to think of rivulets refreshing bugs under logs, stones and pebbles, sinking down to roots...dragging Kentucky Fried Chicken packaging and shit down efficient drains.

I'd sat down again by the time the woman would have reached The Angel. I searched through my favourite sounds for something suited to my mood: synth piano, synth strings, cello. FANTASY 1 AND 2 were particular favourites back then. The rhythms I used most often were NEW JACK SWING and EURO BEAT. Awful names. I usually set the tempo, ranged from 40-240 beats per minute, to low. Nice and slow. It was a rare occasion when I didn't use the out jack to deliver the output to the tape recorder in my stereo.

I'd never had a problem with my Yamaha, not once.

The merry-go-round of insincerity started off with phone calls, exploratory dialogue.

"He's not up yet but I'll give him a shout. Hold on," said Stephen's mother.

A bell-ringing budgie could be heard in the background, talking rubbish.

"Hello?"

"Hi." (Pause) "This is..." (Slightest pause) "...Bike Boy." I hadn't suffered a three year teacher-training course, specialising in drama, without some gains.

"Oh, hi! Sorry. Just woken up and I'm still half asleep."
Over the next few minutes his groggy voice would steadily
climb the scale in camp. "What kind of bike have you got?"
"A Rock Hopper Comp. Cantilever brakes, thick knobby
Cannibal tyres and all the gear from Avis in Clerkenwell."
"Oh, I know the shop. You've got a lovely voice,
really...Oh, hold on."
Mother was on the prowl. "Sorry. You still there?"
"Yep."
"You went all quiet."
I took the direct approach: "So, want to meet up? Any
suggestions?"
"Do you go to any of the places on Old Compton Street?"
"Not if I can help it. You're in Richmond. Kew Gardens
is near. We could meet by the main gates."
"What if it's raining? And in the gear?"
"If it rains, Stephen, we get wet."
Then he did it for the first time. His squishy titter. Gluey
bubbles of fluid forced and sucked through clenched teeth.
"Well," I continued, "can you think of an alternative?"
During a silence in which I imagined him enjoying long
masturbatory sessions with the aid of three mirrors
whenever his mother was out, Stephen's brain ticked over.
"No, that'll be fine. Just hope the weather's good."
"Okay. Let's say Friday then. Good Friday. Main gates
at noon. There's just one thing though Stephen."
(Quickly/anxious/interested) "Yeah?"
(GBH manner) "I'll only wait till a quarter past. If
you're more than fifteen minutes late I'll assume you've
chickened out and I'll be off."
Felt I was botching it up. But he was loving it, he told
me so when we met up. Again he laughed. That breathy,
soppy-mouthed short inhaling-exhaling gasping laugh.
"Hey," he said, shifting gear. "What are you, kind of,
you know...*into*?"
"Well Stephen, since you ask, I'm an apprentice serial
killer. I'm hoping you're going to help me get started with
the most *historic* statistic. One of my new year's resolutions
was to kill a human being."

That laugh. Squelch, squelch, squelch. Maybe he hadn't heard of Colin Ireland's realised dream.

"Noon then," he agreed, smiling. "Come rain or shine."

"Come rain or shine, Stephen."

I terminated, pressing a finger down hard. He didn't even know my name. (This is normal.)

Lifting the finger I dialled my next potential victim. 0181-422 ——, Phu Mok in South Harrow. The phone rang for ages before being picked up. The cockney accent came as a shock, I thought I had the wrong number for a minute.

"'Ello?"

"Phu?"

"Just a sec."

The phone was picked up a minute later. At the other end I could hear someone breathing. Nothing was said.

"Mr Mok?"

"Speaking."

An aged yet sparkling voice with more of an American accent than Chinese.

"Hi." (Pause) "This is..." (Slightest pause) "...Bike Boy." "Well! Hello. Thank you so very much for calling," said almost gasping, another one at it. "How nice. Er, when can we meet up?" (Keen.) "I am so looking forward to seeing you." (Very keen.) "I'm so pleased to hear your voice. I really am. When can you come over?" (Desperate.)

He sounded like lots of money.

"When do you suggest, Mr Mok?"

"Right now would be lovely. Would you? Could you?"

Did he think I was a new recruit at his usual escort service?

"Oh, I'm probably rushing you. Forgive me. Um... maybe I should think of a time when we could...you know..."

"How about tea-time on Good Friday?"

Having dispensed with one cycle fetishist I could travel north for a little light refreshment, meeting another.

"Good Friday, yes. Now that would put the *Good* in it. I'll be in all day. All day. It's so nice to hear your young voice. It *really* is. So many of these advertisers are timewasters, you know. Yes, I'm *so* looking forward to seeing you."

"In my shiny black skin-tight cycle shorts."

"Oh, you sweet monster, yes! I'm so looking forward to the vision of you. Shall we say fourish then...and what do I call you? Love you calling me Mr Mok. It's so very..."

I knew exactly what it was and the effect it was having.

"Call me..." (slightest pause, continuing in a whisper) "...call me Bike Boy."

"Actually I really like that, it's so..."

I knew exactly what it was, cheap and instant.

"Got a pen? I'll give you my address. No, silly me. You have it, of course. Well, let me give you directions then."

"Save the dictation, Mr Mok. I have an A-Z."

"Oh, you do sound like a cheeky chap! I am so looking forward to meeting you. You sound like quite a handful!"

"Fantasies become reality on Good Friday at four."

Again I terminated.

They were all so keen to meet Bike Boy. Leading the way, they followed so easily. Any questions asked of me were teasingly deflected. All that mattered was that I came across as a sane, semi-erect, genuine and discreet large penis owner with nothing infectious to worry about. It was like making arrangements for someone else. Not myself.

Jack in Hampstead, an architect with a faintly Scottish accent, anarchic sense of humour and occasional smoker's cough, was fixed in the diary for Bank Holiday Monday. His place, four. I'd decided I would probably go ahead and have some sort of sexual experience. Allan, supposedly sixteen, was eating toast when I phoned. He was slotted in for the Tuesday, by the Peter Pan statue in Kensington Park Gardens. That was enough to be getting on with, easy as ordering pizza. Phoning the others from the *Yes* and *Maybe* selections, I said I was off on a week's cycling tour of Devon and would contact them upon my return. They loved the idea of Bike Boy braving the elements, alone in a tent by the sea. Boy Scout appeal. I had a long chat with Charles of Brockley. Bike Boy was to have his portrait done. I didn't know what to wear.

It was time to acquire a whole new skin, time to go

shopping.

Morning

The downward-looking me knew that shopping was not enough: there were so many disparities between that reflection in the dusty upturned changing room mirror and the smiling Campagnolo team in the poster taped to the back of the door. Sharp, defined, glowing, with shining smooth legs glistening in the sunlight, they were a total contrast to me in that tiny cubicle in the basement of the Clerkenwell Road cycle shop that stank of damp and oil.

Unlike the cycle racing team in the Ever-Ready vests, I had shoulder-length hair, worn loose that day, plus horribly hairy arms and legs. I looked heavy, weighed down and uncomfortable. To make the transformation into fantasy Bike Boy I had to do much more than shop.

My bike was spot on. I'd bought it from the same place only weeks before on a day I vowed never to use London Transport again. Selecting the right cycle shorts took longer than choosing the maximum protection Oakley "M Frames"; the leather-palmed fingerless gloves; the sky-blue Giro helmet; the black baseball cap; the white Sidi socks (which hardly covered my ankles) and the black and blue Sidi Dominator shoes complete with ratchet straps. I tried on nine pairs of shorts in all, like some sort of pedantic fetishist. Eventually I got a perfect fit, like they were made for me: 80% Poliamide, 20% Elastan, made in Italy. Gorgeous.

I didn't like the tops. They all looked too much with the shorts, like a uniform. I chose a silver-grey racing vest from a bargain box, purely because the rayon sheen was like lightning. There wasn't much in the line of cotton but I wasn't worried. I had an idea at the back of my mind.

Funnily enough, it was while hooking up a new water bottle to the bike frame that I felt the first step into character. I could imagine sunlight, heat, summer thirst; light glinting off my glasses as I swallowed noisily, watched by someone, somewhere, some time in the near future.

In the shop I absorbed new information like an actor going through the Stanislavskian approach. Gears by

Shimano, Japanese. A Flite saddle. I'd chosen a larger than average frame, 23`, got myself a 'D' lock—before I'd just thought of it as a big black thing that was a bugger to get the knack of. I could name-drop. I'd acquired sexy smokescreen language.

The large wrap-around Oakley glasses had the effect of a black mask. When I put them on I kind of blanked. I liked the feeling.

Afternoon

"Yeah, I know what you mean. Elvis looked his best then, you're right. So, a number two at the back, tapering up to a three here, longer on top, bit longer than a flat-top, even longer at the front, like so. And the sideburns to...here? Right. I'll just get you washed."

Rox was an Old Compton Street poof parlour where Soho habitués used to get their regimented looks crafted. It was my first haircut in three years. I wanted to look like Elvis when he joined the army, a tall order. Shaun, a black guy, Irish name and ginger dreadlocks, suggested a surplus of oil to give it a sheen once the clipping and fussing had finished.

The transformation really kicked in when his fingers pulled the oil back over my skull, darkening the thick, dark brown to black in an instant. I suddenly looked sharper, intensified and younger. Marketable.

Evening

As well as cutting out dairy products, I'd planned to swim daily but changed tactics in the queue at Ironmonger Row Baths, taking the lazy option of booking in for six sun-bed sessions instead. Enriching the tan I'd picked up escaping a family Christmas, alone on a rooftop in Tunisia, brought me closer to the Bike Boy image my idle mind had created.

Wearing Speedos to preserve my tan line, prostrate between two layers of blue-white bulbs, I felt like an Apollo astronaut about to be launched into infinity.

Night

Sporting the M Frames and white Calvin Kleins, I watched my reflected body tease through air, blank and comfortable and new, standing without expression for a long time in the privacy of my bedroom.

The M Frames, according to the colour brochure, possessed innovative features, accommodating every head size and shape with an ingenious Hammer Earstem. Unobtanium earsocks worked in conjunction with the nosepieces to grip my head tenaciously, yet comfortably, at nose and temples. Unobtanium is hydrophylic: it gets sticky as it becomes moist with sweat, helping the frames to stay put no matter how hard you run, ski or jerk off.

Even before meeting anyone, I decided on placing five more Bike Boy adverts, varying the wording to make them more teasing, more enticing. I wanted more letters, a continual response. Dirty little secrets were something to get up in the morning for. I wanted to be in a position to select and, more excitingly, reject.

Once again I filled out the coupons, thirty spaces for a maximum of thirty words. These were mailed, second class, every other day and placed in a variety of sections. I was to become quite a little earner for the Chronos Group. The replies would stink to an extent I could not have imagined. Maybe I wanted to encounter people worse off than myself as some sort of consolation.

BIKE BOY! LEGS: Muscular. BODY: Slim.
SKIN: Smooth. SMILE: Wicked. HAIR/
EYES: Dark. PECTORALS: Pronounced.
BICEPS: Bulging. BUTTOCKS: Firm.
AGE:22. NAME: Liam. (Uncut. WE.)
Seeking Ad-venture! Like cycle shorts?

BIKE BOY: Big Boy/Big bike/Big smile/Big
heart of gold/Strong dominant
personality/22/WE. Likes: swimming,
showers, oil, decent films, indecent videos,
Indie, imagination, Hubba Bubba, surprises.

BIKE BOY in shiny black skin-tight cycle shorts will turn fantasies into realities. 22, slim, smooth, athletic, safe. Genuine, discreet and honest. Cute bum, wicked smile. (Horny devil!) Curious? ALA.

BIKE BOY: Mountain bike rider. (Black skin-tight cycle shorts.)22. Long smooth muscular legs. WE. "Cute". Likes: cycling downhill in the rain. Dislikes: Shakespeare/Ballet/Opera. Open to suggestions. ALAWP.

MOUNTAIN BIKE RIDERS? Shiny black skin-tight cycle shorts? I'm tall, slim, smooth, horny. (22). Legs: muscular. Eyes/Hair: dark. (Size 10 feet!) Home alone, EC1. Seeking social intercourse ASAP. Interested?

Passing through Piccadilly on my way to Clone Zone to pick up the gaypers, I had the pleasure of walking behind a young body poured into denim. It was the lower half which was of interest. I followed along Shaftesbury Avenue, close to limbs in motion. If the body had been cut at the waist I'd still have followed the remains in fascination. A cut at the calf muscles would have been good too, losing those cowboy boots, leaving the two heaviest and strongest bones in the body to continue, as if walking on air. Femurs, my favourites.

It wasn't the arse which made me quicken my step to catch up, but the small hips and outer upper thighs. As one leg lifted, the other stepped down. I watched muscles I don't know the names of contract, then relax. Contract, then relax. These human parts were of shapes and proportions I wanted to touch, so lovely as they moved. Perhaps even lovelier stilled. When I overtook, I didn't turn back to see the face that headed it all, though the idea of glimpsing his packet, cocooned in denim, urged me to. I'd got to the point where I didn't care if someone caught me staring.

My favourite shelf-filler at Sainsbury's noticed me as he replenished the broccoli section. He was growing his hair. Maybe the expense of regular flat-tops was a financial consideration. It suited him longer. I remembered the day I'd seen him shopping in the bakery section with his mother, seeming years younger in the role of son. He'd caught me looking at him then, too, and blushed, pretending to be bored. Maybe he was. I'm sure I wasn't his only admirer.

I've still got a feeling I'll bump into him somewhere one of these days and when that day comes he'll momentarily blush and perspire just enough to be exciting, then look pissed off and turn away. Who knows, he might even smile, might say hello. Hello at the London Apprentice, Sub Station or the Anvil where he would lean back against a wall to porno mumble "Go on then, suck it!"

I wondered, as I did so often, about his chest.

Home in time for the nine o'clock news.

Twice that night I found myself struggling with a hard-on which hurt. My tongue wanted to meet warm wet lips and another soft mouth. My nipples wanted fingernails and teeth. My cock just ached to come any old how. Both times I totted up the minutes and energy tokens it would take to put on jeans, boots, Ray's old leather jacket and, second to the bike ride in terms of time management, shave. A fresh face isn't necessary for success in the shadows of a back room, but I didn't know that then. The Block, a jerk off establishment up by Angel tube, opposite Sainsbury's—a place I'd avoided hearing much about—was the one place on Earth my dick was begging to be taken.

While lorries rumbled, taking the best of British beef to Smithfield Market, I wanked like an adolescent, thinking of those limbs encased in denim and the shelf-filler whose hands had touched what I'd eaten and the mystery of his chest and the smell of the small of his back, those eighteen-year-old eyebrows and that voice I once heard talking to a mate on the subject of fake Armani jeans—I reached a violent, noisy orgasm as I imagined licking his thick, black neck. By the time I would have been paying the admission fee to join the herd at The Block, I was asleep.

I'd set the alarm, expecting another batch of letters. The postman had no trouble with the envelope this time, dead on eight thirty.

Someone at *Boyz* had made a mistake. An envelope was marked for Box NS465 but with a six that looked like a zero. I did the decent thing, returning it to their office with a second-class stamp as soon as I'd read it. The communication in large capital letters showed admirable economy:

I WANT TO BE YOUR HUMAN TOILET
0171 230 ——Mark

A Westminster code. Maybe a nice, respectable button-down shirt sort of a chap with a combination lock briefcase. Perhaps a lusty lawyer, a company medic, a bank manager, butcher, or toilet attendant.

Starting the day with a photocopied letter from Chris over in Nine Elms would have sent most people back to bed. For his 5``x7`` self-portrait, this leather queen had attempted the studio look, draping white bed-sheets in a corner as a backdrop. Edging into the picture, providing an insight into his other world, was a patterned carpet—granny variety—in grotesque reds and browns. I suppose one advantage was it wouldn't show blood, except to a forensic team.

God bless his shiny black knee-length motor-cycle boots. God love his super white socks rolled over the tops. God help him in those black leather trousers just that bit too tight in an effort to be sensuous.

Studded wristbands added to his discomfort and a badge-covered leather and denim waistcoat gaped open, revealing various weights dangling from huge, pierced nipples. Nipples the size of a lactating dalmation's. Nipples with the tough density of warts. Below his left bicep was a once discreet sacred heart which over the years had evolved into a complex skulls-and-daggers affair stretching halfway down his arm. Above it an eagle or phoenix rose up out of flames—loads of yellow and stars—perhaps reflecting an interest in animal wildlife. A certain empathy with endangered species.

Tight, black leather: pressing, restricting and restraining every inch, wrapping him like a samosa, muscles firmly encased. Eyes giving the camera that long thick dick look, mind adrift in a sea of seminal fluid. A photo full of...something...not raunch. God bless and save him.

The mass-distributed photocopy read:

Hi,
saw your advert and felt it was time to answer one after all these years of reading. I am forty years of age, fit and able. My main interests are leather and all it entails. I have plenty of gear, accoutrements, toys etc. Am into jocks, shorts, etc etc. Like oil massage, safe sex, have some experience with Domination, S&M or whatever. Brand new video with exciting tapes sits awaiting your arrival. Photo taken only last week. 0171 498 —— for a fab time. (Beware of the answerphone.)

Chris.
(Safe Sex Stud.)

Verdict: No chance. Not a hope in hell.

Sitting on his leather Chesterfield, darkest green velvet curtains soaking up the light, Ikea bookcase bursting with impressive reading, he looked like a nice chap. Though concerned about his gut (holding his stomach in like a collector's item pin up) he managed a smile.

The beer gut would have been less obvious if he'd been clothed. A circumcised gentleman who'd felt more than just the one surgeon's knife. Again, the intimacy and stillness of a self-timer photograph, shot with available light. I wondered what the reject photos had looked like.

On a plain postcard he'd laid down his particulars in more huge capitals.

MOTTO: Pain Is Pleasure
AIM: To Experience Pleasure
LIKES: Smooth Skinned Muscular Types
AGE: 40
BUILD: 5`11`` / 11 Stone / Moustache
NAME: Paul
TEL: 0171 813 ——

Verdict: N-O. The intensity of one self-timed photo after another was wearing.

The amount of feeling and crafting which had gone into presenting each image, at such expense of time, energy and pocket, was remarkable.

From perhaps only a ten minute walk away came an intelligent hand and an astounding outpouring on two A4 sheets of economy file.

#–, Block ——
—— Estate
—— Street
London N1
0171 704 ——

Hi,

I liked your provocative and enticing ad in *Boyz*. Your physical description is certainly eye-catching. I actually own black, skin-tight cycle shorts, currently idle in my room as a token to my once obsessive hobby. Yes—I do like them!

My name is PJ. I'm 28, 6´1´´, weigh 11 stone and have a slim physique. I have enclosed a photograph that will flesh out this description.

I am a newcomer to London, having grown up in Northern Ireland and in the last two years travelled through Europe with the bold ambition of eventually visiting every country on Earth. I originally came to London simply to raise cash, but I have since decided to settle here, find a job and a place to stay, reconsidering my future. At the moment I'm staying with my sister just off Essex Road, Islington.

My job is defined as Hotel Night Porter. Not great pay but I get by. I work in rotation so on alternate fortnights I'm free to do as I like. Movies are my great escape from the routine of daily existence. This is the first and singular passion in my life and to some extent casts a shadow over my other interests. I read *Empire* and *Première* each month though don't really take much notice of the critics. Who does?

Music means more to me than just background noise. There are only a few artists whose entire work I love: U2, Simple Minds, Peter Gabriel, REM—but I'm more into singles than albums—nothing beats a great new song.

This is the first time I've actually sought to meet people and it feels odd to sell myself so candidly, but there is a deeper reason for this than just building up social contacts. To meet a guy who is gay is a major step for me. Without exception all the gay men I have seen in my life have appeared as effeminate, which I loathe. I'm just not like that at all. Living a regular lifestyle, privacy and discretion are extremely important to me and something I won't compromise on, but I need proof that to be gay is not only to be unhappy or camp. Sometimes I think I'm the only straight-acting gay guy in the world. Being gay goes against the grain of my upbringing, religion etc. It'd create hell with my family if they ever found out. (So please be discreet when phoning.)

I don't frequent pubs or clubs; they are just not my scene. Cafes and restaurants are better. Best of all is going out to events, day or night, be it sport, theatre or a concert, and just grabbing a take-away. This is how I would like my social life to be, with a share of movies and quiet nights in (or both). Basically I'm looking for a guy of like mind and heart. A boyfriend (how strange and wonderful that sounds to me). A friend and a lover. The two of us trying to figure this world out. It's difficult to present you with a picture of myself that, however imperfect, is truthful without being superficial. If I have given you some idea of who I am and how I feel then this letter has been worthwhile and hopefully will strike a chord with you and impel you to reply.

If you would like to meet me, please reply to the address below. Just a short note would do (with a photo of you in cycle shorts?) If we don't seem compatible I'll understand, but would you please let me know.

Yours faithfully,
PJ Healy

Verdict: Lovely letter, probably a very nice guy, but uh uh. I didn't want to pricktease anyone with a drop of sincerity in them, anyone I could have had some chance with. I just wanted to feed upon and be fed into the dreams of the not so nice one-timers.

The majority of respondents would have benefited from tips on how to play the game in ad-land. Some of the scraps of stationery weren't fit to be bird-cage liners. As for the writing and horrific choice of photographs enclosed, well, I felt like phoning a few of them up just to put them on the right lines. Getting them on the right lines, of course, might have required a referral to a structured therapy programme at the Portman Clinic, the Maudesley, PACE or some such place.

From the toilet seat I could see the letter-box, external flap up, letting in the usual smelly breeze. It was this which finally got me moving.

The balcony overlooked a post office, a Chinese take-away, an Indian take-away, an off-license, some sort of everything-you-could-possibly-want-for-your-car shop, a general store, a bus stop, a pub called the Shakespeare's Head, a one-way street in which traffic went further and further away, and a triangle of sky. Ray and I once had people round on Guy Fawkes Night. It wasn't a great view. Two or three floors up it was probably something.

Returning to the bedroom for another four hours, slightly scared, I lay stewing: my scalp hurt. I thought I had a brain tumour. Later on I got the hoover out and reached into every corner like a good boy.

In the privacy of my minimum involvement accommodation, I was an unhappy independent. I could have been dead in there for weeks before anyone would have suspected, more weeks still before anything was done about it. Only the smell would bring police intervention, as is so often the case.

Good Friday.

It looked like spring had finally got going. All over London people were getting on with a spot of decorating. I felt triumphant, mine was all done. The pores of my skin were feeling the change in the weather.

Hair removal was as per instructions on the Immac spray can. I used a GII for the final tidy-up job—discouraged in the instructions. An invitation to irritation. Even those little hairs around my arse got a careful spray of the lemon-scented stuff. As stringent with my body as with my interior decorating, I got down to the business of cutting fingernails and toenails right back. Three different toothbrushes, each with all-important functions, went into action.

As I was lying in the bath, all kinds of memories hit me. My scars were apparent, silvered on my hairless skin. I remember the day the incisions were made. I insisted on watching. Tubes were inserted to filter in blue dye before the repeated back-and-forth scanning. That dye gave me a fabulous blue-grey complexion for a year—the total cancer victim look. I don't fill out a pair of Levi's the way I used to, having only the one testicle. Lying there, still, water cooling, I must have looked like a piece of performance art.

I was early, prepared as if for an audition. Coach loads of tourists were doing Kew. Placing my bike upside down beside me, I sat, then lay, on a chained-in area of lawn near the cricket pitch by the entrance, wondering if prisoners ever sunbathe. With the peak of my cap turned round to the back I did my best to strike an erotic pose, lying down beside my bike, head on pannier, making believe the sun was a spotlight trained on me.

Over the years I'd blagged a lot of teeshirts out of PRs. When I'd successfully acquired one, it would be stored away in polythene for a special future time. That time had come. For each rendezvous I'd wear a different teeshirt, fresh as the day it was wrapped. They became part of the ritual, more individual than the shiny rayon available at Avis Cycles.

That day I wore a Blur teeshirt. Nothing special, just B-L-U-R in silver grey on powder blue. Being an XL it came to just below crotch level. Teasing. The clothes, bike and preened body felt more perfect than awkwardly new. I waited with my eyes shut.

I was made aware of Stephen's presence first by the gentle click of his well oiled chain, then by a cooling shadow over my face. I ignored him for a while, then opened pretend-sleepy eyes; he was tall, backlit and nervously excited. It was boredom at first sight.

Setting a time limit at the outset, I explained to Stephen

that I had to meet up with friends for tea later. It laid a foundation of tension which I enjoyed and established my power to dictate the pace of events. The subtle gradation of power in this first rendezvous was soon to be taken for granted. There was a conflict of desires: to me this young Stephen was just the first of many human specimens to tease, while I felt that to him I was, at first anyway, some sort of possibility.

That mouth of his: a shallow, narrow cavity, low roofed, with over-active salivary glands flooding it to brimming. Possibly sweet, clear saliva. His speech was impaired accordingly, the stomach-turning feature in an otherwise acceptable, usable body.

In the Temperate House that mouth told me Stephen's fascinating life story. Maybe I was mean not to offer him a shoulder to cry on. In the Tropical House the same mouth babbled on about what turned him on. Almost certainly I was rotten not to wink him towards the Gents to let him wet my dick. And he *was* turned on, I could tell, but trying hard to look bored. Perhaps more obvious than the occasional sexual excitement evident in the lycra shorts was his acute self-consciousness at being head to toe in favourite erotic get-up while the perfect excuse for wearing it all was chained to the railings by the main gates.

Eating ice-cream back on the grass where we'd met— distanced from the crowds—he moved in for the kill.

"You've got lovely legs."

"Thank heavens for Immac," said I.

This clouded his face.

"That's what my mum uses," he said disapprovingly.

I quickly pursued this small route of discomfort, hoping to turn him off as easily as I'd turned him on.

"Do you believe in reincarnation?" I asked.

Squelching an awkward laugh, he didn't have an answer.

"It's just that...I've been wondering, if there is such a thing as reincarnation, what do you reckon Joe Orton came back as?"

"That's a bloody weird thing to come out with," he sprayed.

After that I felt relief as the mutual discarding process began. I was glad when he started whining on about his boyfriend and the problems they were having. How he didn't want to move in, how he didn't want to be *out*. How he didn't fancy the relentless clubbing, the Es, being peed on.

I finally shook him off with the "I'll call you up sometime" line. We both knew I wouldn't and I didn't.

I was fifteen minutes early. Someone sat, back turned, in the PS-worthy garden. I rang my bike bell instead of the doorbell and walked straight in, wheeling my bike over the lawn to lean it against a cherry tree in full bloom. The turning figure, mid-to-late forties, grey crop, was the cockney.

"Didn't think you'd come," he said, smiling like I was a long-haul passenger about to be strip-searched at Customs. "I'm Eric, by the way."

I nodded with a weak smile, like I'd arrived for a job interview that I'd changed my mind about. Taking a seat in a worn wicker chair, knowing it would line my arse through the lycra, I could smell him and he smelled nice. He'd recently been working with wood or putty. He rubbed a thick wrist over his unshaven face as I put on the teeshirt I'd removed at the end of the road to make a bare-chested entrance.

"Blur," he said. "Crap if you ask me."

"That Damon's pretty shaggable though, don't you think?"

It was a shame Mok was about, I would have quite happily lowered my arse on Eric's face providing he shaved first. We sat without smalltalk, enjoying five minutes of blue sky through the fruit trees. The lawn was a battlefield, not mown but butchered—torn short.

I heard Mok before I saw him, smelled his hairspray before I felt his soft hands in a firm handshake. Encased head to toe in his favourite cycle fetish gear he was a hideous sight. His Ever-Ready top was a sad contrast to the poster in the basement changing room. The lycra only emphasised the cargo of his unpleasantly collected anatomy.

I turned the peak of my cap to the front for a moment, then back again nervously. The old poof liked all that. Relaxing into the back of his chair, Mok let his guts sag out and down, slipping over the top of his cycle shorts.

"You look absolutely lovely. I'd very much like to suck you off," he announced.

I gave him an empty glare for a good five seconds then looked away towards the garden gate. After a fit of coughing he enquired about the response to my ad, whether other cyclists had replied and if they'd sent pictures. I said nothing at first, then:

"One. I'd like a hot, sweet, weak cup of tea, asap. With biscuits. Two. Give me a tour of your house, keeping your hands off me. Three. Tell me the story of your fascinating life. Four. Make an imaginative indecent proposal within the hour."

Just one whiff of indoors and I knew there were mouse turds in the pantry. Tea was served in Minton in a dining-room cluttered with Queen Anne chairs and gilt frames. The decor swayed between vulgarity and piss elegance. There was a ridiculous time travel feeling to the place. Mok was dying for a lick of my arse up against the Fleur-de-lis flocking. In his head he was fine-tuning for my ears the indecent proposal he'd made so many times.

When I'd had two sips of tea and a custard cream, he led me up a staircase, walls covered with photographs by a fancy French photographer who'd died of the big disease with a tiny name. Waterfalls, rivers, lakes—at dusk or dawn. Stilled waters. A hesitation on the first floor landing; from the window the cockney's shadow could be seen hosing down a wall.

"Maybe I should explain the situation here. My friend."

"The cockney."

"Yes, Eric. Well, we are *not* lovers. *Not* a couple, *not* together—though we *were* a long time ago. He's my housekeeper, makes things tick along nicely, keeps things shipshape. Keeps trouble at bay."

I was more intrigued at the mention of "trouble".

"We met over thirty years ago when it wasn't legal, or

lethal. You know. Well, although young, fancying a bit, I didn't mind paying. Boys were dirt cheap then. I was his first punter and he was my first rent-boy."

His eyes sparkled like there was proposition in the air and a condom on the bedside table. I'll show you mine, if you'll show me yours. To avoid smirking I looked away at undergarments of mythic proportions on a clothes line next-door. Mok came from another time, a time when servants blackmailed having overheard a conversation, read a discarded letter, or found beneath a pillow a strand of young, full-coloured hair.

The master bedroom was dominated by a four poster *Antiques Roadshow* would happily give a couple of minutes to. Shutting all three sets of curtains his mother had chosen in happier times (when England was a green and pleasant land), he eyed me with practised speculation: *Can I get him to do it?* The copulating rhythm of the universe began to pound in that room which had the not unfamiliar stink of a used booth in a Times Square porno emporium. He wanted a nice slow quickie as he turned the key in the door.

"I do hope you're going to kill me," I said, at a volume just above a schoolboy's seductive whisper.

He turned to me and smiled. Expensive dentistry seemed to glow in the dark. Switching on a bedside table lamp which instantly started to burn dust, he winked me toward a bookcase crammed with every kind of queer shit.

A sperm-fest of treasure which is not, according to the Obscene Publications Act (1956), supposed to sail so readily through letter-boxes all over the UK—hardcore. Thank heavens for foreign magazines. *Suck, Hard, Jock, Inches, Torso, Blue Boy, Chicos, Rump, Skinflicks, Honcho, Playguy* and many many more lined the shelves. Pretty boys, not so pretty boys and muscle men with enormous knockers and shaved butt-holes. How many subscription forms had this man filled out in his time? A time that ranged from the birth of the posing pouch to the fruits of the Regulation catalogue. *Body Beautiful* (Studies in Masculine Art) 35¢, 2/6 and *Adonis* (The Art Magazine of Male Physique) 35¢, 2/6, lay in two neat piles, exposing frayed spines.

On the walls were prints of paintings from the late-nineteenth century 'aesthetic' school. The subjects: young working class men by water, ready for action. Rowdy crews of East End lads, stripped for the plunge. Boys being boys in the hot summer months, full of fun, some with mouths parted voicelessly. Boys being boys in the delicious hot summer months, golden skinned, slender and tight. Idyllic and innocent of compulsive workouts, weights and piercings, joyfully splashing, wet. Mates grinning spontaneously, looking into each other's eyes, happy in their warm congregations, not a designer label or naff tattoo on them. Cool after the water but warming nicely in the sun, costumes clinging to every curve and bulge. Sun kissed—and wanked over by a 'mountain bikist' in South Harrow.

What a business it must have been to sustain that (estimated) three-mags-one-video-a-week handjob habit of his. The expense of it all. He probably also logged on to all the websites flogging big dick holograms.

He had a Dunkirk spirit when it came to orgasms, a real fighting determination to conquer cocks. I wondered how many buckets of spunk had soaked him one way or another over the years. They say spunk's good for the skin, it hadn't worked for that one. Bet he got busy with tit clamps, bottle of poppers and a latex real feel dildo the size of a baby-doll up his arse every once in a while. I know about men like him and their cheques don't bounce.

As I flicked through a vintage copy of *Vulcan*, a certain *Randy Ray* in a wet teeshirt and little else, spreadeagled over a motorbike, almost jumped off the page at me. Ray had said he'd done a couple of wank mags when he first hit London. I hadn't believed him, but the poppable pimples on his forehead and bum, undisguised with make-up, were so Ray. I suppose I went all quiet.

Mok was busy with the video he'd chosen in anticipation of another lovely wank and final suck off. Some pornographic slapstick called *The Hollywood Kid* starring Rock Hardon. America's clean-limbed youth all coming alive with a press of the *PLAY* button.

A sizeable penis shot a wad of liquid genetics over a

blond boy's butt in the slow motion technique engineers have worked so hard to perfect throughout the twentieth century; soundtracked with homosexy oinks and grunts laid over a 130 bpm tune. Definitely too much for James Ferman and his colleagues at the British Board of Film Classification.

"Now, this is a *really really* lovely piece of action. Double plus good!" said Mok, sitting on the bed.

"Hey!" he whispered, head tilted coquettishly, patting the bedspread only to send dog hair flying into the air. "Sit next to me. Let's pretend we're in some filthy little cinema."

He stared through the tv, hoping I'd soon be requiring relief. My penis, skin and capillary plus erectile tissue just like any other, was the one penis in this world he was desperate to have banging the phlegm beyond his tonsils.

An erect penis has the smooth, tight skin of a child. An erect penis has the look of an astronaut, ready to venture forth where no man has ever been...or not for a while anyhow. It implies speed, power, transience. When limp the flaccid penis folds back, turns in upon itself, trailing off (sighing). Wrinkly and lined, like a fingerprint.

When I sat next to Mok he smiled like he'd just been found not guilty on sixteen separate charges, displaying teeth, tongue and tonsils with absolutely no dental self-consciousness, furry candida thriving.

"What do you like best: anal, oral or straight penetration?" he asked with the banality that can only come from repeated over-exposure. I felt his breath on my face as the credits of fake names rolled. Only the very largest financial incentive might have made me get close, laughing at the whole situation as he sucked me off on arthritic knees. As I was thinking this, I saw the fountain pen, cheque card and open cheque book on top of the tv. He winked a zip eye. This strategy must have turned many a fantasy into an affordable (gettable) reality.

Explicit camerawork: four eyes watched sweat ooze from teenage pores as the pain of lost virginity was faked.

Mok was desperate for me to make the first move. Perhaps sensing that I'd happily bludgeon him to death with the baseball bat (a miniature version of a Louisville Slugger) kept under his bed for other purposes, he sat on his hands. I'm sure those stubby fingers wanted to make an inventory of my vertebrae. And I'm sure that beside his miniature baseball bat was a plastic bag containing Enlargo Cream, Stop & Erecta Cream, Stud Delay & Action Spray and a Mr Perfection strap-on double dong. Plus a Jumbo dildo, a Rambo Dildo, and—*a full eight inches of real-feel latex shaped and veined just like the real thang to bend and rotate inside you!*—a shiny new Squirmy Rooter.

"Well, Mr Mok, the clock's ticking by. It's time for you to truly amaze me. I want you to shock me, make me wonder. Time to make an imaginative indecent proposal."

He looked disappointed and challenged. Normally he'd have been wearing a pubic moustache by that point.

"Okay, Bike Boy, I have just the thing, something you'll remember for the rest of your life."

Leaving his pornography heaven we climbed two flights of stairs to an attic, followed by an alsatian who stared at me with old brown eyes.

"You let yourself in, I'll just go and get myself ready."

There was a long, narrow room behind that heavy torture chamber door. The room was like a Tudor hall. I took the initiative of lighting all three candelabra. Gilt chairs with red velvet seats waited, one sized for Mok's derrière.

"This is Pogo," he whispered, hugging a large white cat to his chins. "Always up and down on things. That's Puddles," he said kicking the alsatian, which tore down three flights of stairs on nails in need of clipping.

He took a bottle of poppers out of his white leather jock strap, the only item of clothing he was now wearing.

"It would so excite me if you lowered your shorts and played with yourself a bit," he said unscrewing the little brown bottle.

Sitting his fat arse down with deacon-like poise, he looked at me pleadingly, taking four deep sniffs.

"Oh, go on. Be a love and drop 'em like a naughty good boy. Let's get a look," he said, stroking his crotch. "Show us your knob."

A proposal lacking erection etiquette, I thought.

He played three French, seventeenth century pieces on three different-sized harps. As his penis hardened, he tiptoed his fingers in show-offy ripples, head and shoulders rashing up. The cat sat on my lap purring. Of course I clapped when he'd finished his showpiece, but that frightened dear Pogo, whose needle-sharp claws lanced into me in his hurry to escape.

Then things began to fizzle. The ball was definitely in my court and I wasn't in the mode to play. The blank space in the cheque book was at my command, but I wasn't ready to enter that arena. Mok sensed I wanted to get the fuck out of there and he admitted defeat graciously.

"Listen, Bike Boy, give me a tinkle one day soon and maybe we can come to, you know, some sort of arrangement. I like you very much. I do." What he wanted was a lick of my arse, warm cum down his throat. Nothing out of the ordinary, really.

The CHORD MEMORY had three separate banks used to store different accompaniments. I used this facility because it was fun, changing chord sequences in a variety of orders. This allowed me to record a verse and chorus in different banks then chain them in the desired order for playback.

Up to eight steps could be programmed. A synthesised voice announced the order of the programmed banks each time a BANK button was pressed. It was very well behaved.

There are lots of other people in this world besides Mr Right. Jack had been sent, had sent himself—to my box number. To me.

I manoevered from front door to bedroom without a word. There we both lay, on his bed, almost identical. Pleading eyes across the pillow wandered over my face and chest. There we both lay, on his bed, both tall, both slim, both smooth, both dark, each with a knee dragged up sideways, facing each other, icily regular. Peaceful, pale flesh on his bed, warm and real and ready. Curtains and windows flung wide open.

When I arrived appearances had it that he was sanding down an old chair but there was no dust on the backs of his hands, no motes in the sunbeams breaking through the bamboo cane blinds. It was all a part of his tough-boy act. His cropped hair, mashed up khaki shorts and tiny black vest too. But once in bed he did that gentle change-around which tough-boys so often do. Slowly unfolding, revealing a sensitive side needing a good fuck.

Having stared at the ceiling as if scared in the minute before he came, he said "Wow!" as the last drop of ejaculate splashed high upon his chest, then smiled too much as I withdrew, whipping off the slimy, shit-free condom to warm his deflating penis with what he'd been waiting for.

After coughing a bit he said, "That's better." Our sperm, dispersed all over him, dried on skin the colour of frosted glass, cool to the touch. I felt the breeze from the open window.

"You're *cute*," he said.

I felt nothing but the breeze.

"You're very cute," he said. I hate that. If there's one thing I'm not, it's *cute*.

He slept soundly, lying still and content. I felt left out. He'd had a happy orgasm and all I'd done was shoot my load to complete the operation. How very trusting he was, I thought, fast asleep with a stranger. How calm he looked after efficient sex.

I pulled the duvet over him. It felt like an unpaid task, so I removed it again before he felt either the warmth or the coldness of sudden loss.

My dick had been inside him but he didn't know my name. Didn't know that his was the first body I'd slept with in the three years since Ray. He probably thought I was just one of the Stepford Boyz. It was out of character to be so random, so easy to be had. He'd kissed every inch of my body, nibbled here and there, dousing me with his saliva. All he'd done was touch my outsides, the skin stretched over the grotesque mess of me. He hadn't made me smile. Ray used to put his arms around me and the warmth was magnificent. Our lovemaking was so much sweeter with the prospect of his death just around the corner. Jack wasn't face-down into a pillow—tied down—but he could have been. No, he was turned towards me sideways, free—in a delicacy of exposure. Pale flesh on the bed. Real and beautiful, trusting. It's a short leap from kissing to killing.

I watched a dribble of his/my/our spunk glide from his navel, missed in the mopping-up operation he'd done with my Madonna teeshirt, saying it was all she was good for. I hadn't found that funny at all.

I spotted two pigeons fucking on the fire escape. Spunk continued to glide down from his navel. Before it hit the poly-cotton bedsheet, I captured it up with the middle finger of my right hand and spread it over his bottom lip, then upper, then over and over in a sideways figure of eight, before lightly plunging inside to smear his two front teeth.

Not a twitch. He was dead to it all. I shivered pale green goosebumps as I took in the bachelor flat around me. Nothing soft about the furnishings, it was clear he preferred severity of surface.

The breeze from the windows pushed the wardrobe door ajar with a squeak. From the breast pocket of a tweed jacket, rimless glasses magnified pale grey woven threads. A dozen or so ties awaited use. Shiny, black HMSO confidential waste bags spilled from a tea chest. Perhaps in a chest beneath a curtain and pages torn from *The Independent*, I might have discovered a skull, an assortment of lungs, kidneys and intestines. Or old throwouts ready for Oxfam.

"Jack," I whispered. "Wakey wakey."

Nothing. Bad Jack.

On the bedside table, next to a cream enamel lamp, stood a box of tissues. Maybe a nasty streak in him chose to ignore them, wanting to defile my teeshirt. Beside the tissues lay a dusty pair of glasses, a Cannon Sureshot camera plus a tube of—of all things—superglue.

I continued to look at his pale flesh without blinking, willing him to wake up. His breathing had slowed right down, like he'd reached a place he was meant to stay. And I the keeper.

It was getting dark. England's even worse when grey

clouds take their usual place in front of the sun. Reaching over his body, armpit to nose, finger to switch, I turned the light on and with rising anger studied a map of previous stains on the sheets.

Pointing the camera at his face I took the first of a series of snapshots. The flash didn't work. This annoyed me. I'd wanted to startle him, but neither the metallic click nor auto-wind woke him. Easing myself down the bed, I framed another portrait shot, then a profile. Sweat had amassed at the nape of his neck, messing his haircut. Click. Then head and shoulders, cut to the waist, a three quarters.

Over by the window, I got a full length. The pigeons flew away. Then I shot a rear view. A much fingered textbook arse: rock hard, boxy with the edges rounded off, inward curving dips creating cute shadows on the sides. *Did I read that somewhere?* Empty eye socket of an arsehole. Bullet hole of an arsehole. Corrupt belly button of an arsehole. *Did I hear that somewhere?* I could imagine an arm disappearing up there, clutching soft warm insides to rip out at the least expected moment. I took pictures which would surely be out of focus, too close in. He was in good shape, musculature many would buy by the pound. I walked, snapping, knowing the pictures would be a blur.

I was hoping he might have opened up an eye quizzically, teasingly, before grabbing me to tickle and laugh like some Hollywood star. Rock Hudson. Or Rock Hardon. But he was miles and miles away. A good hard slap around his face would have been lovelier than that hour of licking. The careful incision of a knife along the jugular or the steady delivery of a weighty syringe was what he merited.

Then he became an object of potential desire again, my own Sleeping Beauty. Listening to the beating heart, then the intestinal music of rising bubbles in his stomach and the slow, deep breathing rekindled my capacity for tumescence.

Whilst he slept so happily with himself, I began to jerk off, hoping for a more satisfactory orgasm. Even with my own porno tableau beside me, I thought of Ray. My Ray. He had a beautiful waist, it really dipped in. He was skin and bone long before the chemotherapy left him skeletal. When laying on his side I used to rub the dip with a karate chop-shaped hand, like I was sawing him. Sex with Ray was gentle, so warm. (Ray, you bastard, I still love you. Can you hear me?)

When my eyes focused into the shaded blackness of horse chestnut branches, a snapshot memory of Ray's black eyes then (surprising me) the shelf-filler's forearms and shiny forehead helped me come streaky splashes up, up, up my chest. Silently. I swamped it all into my navel.

As I lightly spread another figure of eight over his lips, my eyes focused on the superglue. Just a drop between those lips could have shut his mouth for good. With another spreading of my warm slimy cum I touched his nostrils. Outside, then in. Had it been superglue, had I squeezed those nostrils shut, how long would it take for shutdown? Spreading the last of the now cool semen over his lips with my thumb, edging teeth apart to touch his tongue and feel the roof of his mouth, I saw his eyes open.

With the aftershock of orgasm, I shivered another spasm of pale green goosebumps when he looked at me. The shuddering came as a shock, dragging me up. His opened eyes were still, like the restart button had been hit, but the machine had not yet warmed up.

I removed my thumb slowly, rising it up to his nostrils, and down the right side of his face, pausing upon a long narrow scar which I hadn't noticed before. Gliding down to the side of his neck, zig-zagging to the nipple jumping slightly with increased heartbeat, then over to my mouth. I tasted saliva and body salt in a way he mistook for adoration. What I tasted more than him was me.

"Penny for your thoughts," he said.

I smiled, saying nothing.

"Go on, what are you thinking about?"

"The garden of a little house I once stayed in," I said, in a voice which struck me as sounding different from my own. Almost Ray's.

"Where?"

"Crete."

"Which part?"

"Just outside Palaiokhora."

"You angel," he said, coughing.

He kissed me on the forehead, then got up to make strong espresso in a mouldy coffee pot. By the time I got back that night I'd practically forgotten the existence of the body in Hampstead. The stains on Madonna's face were boil-washed away as I phoned men I didn't know with my nicest voice and manners.

The sky was identical to that of the morning Ray went into Barts to die. People were busy again after the bank holiday weekend. I stood and stared, had nothing to do.

Ray's back was turned to me. He was just wearing baggy old underpants, standing in his usual spot by the drain-pipe. I stood behind him, holding in the tears. He looked so sparrow. His body had always been precious to him, great and abundant. We could both feel his nourishing blood pump gently away, reducing his strength with the flow.

One day demolition men would go about their work with cranes, drills and heavy hammers, pounding through partitions, lifting blocks, ripping out ironwork, reducing the block of flats to piles of raw materials to be sold for scrap, recycled or dumped—he'd said. The bulldozers of the site-levellers would tidy away before men with brooms appeared. Housewives would wipe their windowsills free of dust, then there'd be nothing left.

It was the same soiled white sky as Ray's last day at the flat, three years back. The grey of that view had invaded me with the fragile existence of those quickly thrown-up quickly pulled-down buildings that nobody loved.

The smell of the coffee made only an hour ago was already fading.

The lights were green from Tottenham Court Road to Marble Arch. I covered Oxford Street in seven minutes, dodging the occasional lemming shopper. Coming off Bayswater Road I dismounted, obeying the 'no cycling' signs in eroded white on grey.

I'd forgotten how theatrical the position of the Peter Pan

statue was. Trying to look normal, I walked through the low gate, up two steps, entering the crazy-paved circular surround of the statue. The bronze of the rabbits, doves, snails and mice had been lightened with frequent touchings of tiny fingers. Areas at the base had also been rubbed bright by the bums of little ones posing for cameras.

I sat for a moment on a bench down by the water, dark edges inviting me in. Off in the distance was the tall, thin, red brick building of the Household Cavalry Mounted Regiment, where steak-fed young men stripped by windows at night, having learned how to kill during the day. Crows in the branches above—I counted nine—were making a lot of noise squawking.

Time can move so slowly when you're waiting for a stranger. Dabbling ducks and diving ducks, opportunistic feeders, made the most of the granary bread I'd brought with me. One bird crossed from the other bank in a straight line, snapping up feathers as it came. I identified this bird, from a nearby notice board, as a grebe: *'Grebes eat a large quantity of feathers to facilitate the passage of particularly indigestible items, such as fish bones.'*

I turned around a few times as I stood there on the edge, half expecting someone behind to give me a good push in and under, holding me down until the bubbles stopped rising to the surface. Only three mounted police trotted by, wearing fluorescent green tops and blank faces.

By the time the grebe got to me all the bread had gone. I mustered up phlegm from the back of my throat, spitting with B Wing precision. My offering was duly snapped up and swallowed. I returned to the bench and realised it was splattered with bird droppings. I checked the seat of my shorts to be sure I'd escaped any smudges. Although the light was fading fast I kept my Oakleys on. I felt watched.

Two women arrived with a little boy who looked as though a terminal disease was winning against the immune system behind his skin. They sat him on one of the lighter areas of bronze to take a photo, then fed the ducks some stale white bread. As they left, Allan arrived on a skateboard.

The child who'd been warned so many times not to talk to strangers, not to accept sweeties from strangers and not to get into the backs of cars belonging to strangers, beamed first at Allan performing an emergency stop wearing beads and a huge buckled belt on his cut-down Levi's, then at me. A nice, big innocent smile. (So young).

The scrape of board on tarmac flustered the birds and off they went. A skimpy grey vest was half tucked into the back of his jeans. Here he was, my very own three-dimensional, animated *Euro Boy*. For a full five minutes he pretended to be just anybody, leaning against the Peter Pan statue, playing a pocket computer game in a bubble of boredom mixed with absorption. The colour of his skin, pale with pink smudged in, smeared up into the air around him. Something was happening inside my eyeballs. A tiny vial was dissolving in each: the contents first freshened then widened my eyes, making them hungry for glimpses to save and replay. It was a struggle to look away.

To control myself while he decided whether to speak to me, I watched the water as if it were a cinema screen. After what sounded like the end of the world on his pocket game, he sauntered over, skateboard under his arm, and delivered a speech with which he'd often fogged mirrors.

"The age of consent in Japan is thirteen and it's legal for any two people over that age to have sex. In Spain it's twelve. Hi!"

The removal of a fresh pack of chewing gum from a front pocket depleted what I'd taken to be this fierce child diva's shapely genitalia by a saddening couple of inches. (Bet that gum was nicely warm, instantly malleable.)

"Hello."

Pointing to my teeshirt he said that he liked Oasis too (unlike myself) and started reeling off details of his musical tastes and bands he'd seen. Disarming and heart warming with his directness, he had the well developed cunning innocence of an embryonic 'dilly boy. No one would have suspected that we were strangers meeting for the first time. He was my fourth encounter, I was his fifth.

He said I looked younger than twenty two. He was

fibbing. I said he looked exactly sixteen, the truth. Too old to be a child star, too young to take leads. No facial hair dimmed his face. His pupils were shrunk to blackheads in the foggy blue. He was high on something and it wasn't Wrigleys.

He had the kind of nipples which didn't know they liked being played with, yet. He was extremely abuser-friendly.

I thought he was admiring my single pannier. He wasn't.

"Oh, Carradice Super C. Very flash! But crap. Mine fell to bits in six months."

From within the flash but crap pannier came two cans of Strongbow. He'd probably have preferred a Hooch.

"To your good health," I toasted, smiling.

While the boy's head rocked back to take a swig, I watched his narrow throat. At last he opened the gum, not offering me any though. The drink went straight to his head and he was off, speaking happily in gloomy negatives about lots of things he hated. His step-father, the National Curriculum, Ecstasy and warts were major concerns.

Most of what he said was aimed at alternate armpits on clear display as he leaned back, arms behind his head. The pose lengthened his body, elongating muscles and giving a lovely definition to the ribcage. Smooth but for a little fuse of fine hair running down from the navel to under the buttons of his Levi's. I imagined a murderer plucking teenage hairs from these armpits, placing them carefully in a self-sealing envelope marked ARMPITS, to complete a set of three—with PUBES and ARSEHOLE so neatly marked in evenly sized capital letters.

From tv, films, extensive secret reading, pool changing room chats and the occasional 0898 phone lines (hard on pocket money in payphones) he knew lots about the wonderful world of sex. He knew of the possibilities open to him and he was impatient. He knew he was attractive and he knew that youth was something up his sleeve.

"Your ad cracked me up! Have you seen mine? It goes something like *Boyish skateboarding boy next door, recently 18. Blond, 5' 9". Slim. Dangerously cute. Inexperienced but keen to learn, seeks...*Well, it varies a bit then, sometimes it says *PE teacher type*. And it ends *Your place, not mine. No clones. No perverts. Photo please. London only.* You know the sort of thing. Sometimes it's over thirty words but they still put it in. They changed the wording once, I suppose it was a bit risky what I wrote. They stuck in words like *masculine, dominant* and *active* instead. Have you seen the ones in *QX*? They're wild."

He was dropping hints with smiling eyes and a tongue which kept his lips moist. Although his voice was croaking a craggy path towards manhood, deep down in a delicate part of himself somewhere he still wanted to be treated as sweetly as baby Jesus. (So easy to destroy.)

He smiled, keeping in his secrets. Every inch was sixteen-year-old perfection, especially the neck: a vulnerable dip at the back, below the graduated hairline, tendons creating a kissable rift. A slender pale neck, delicate and pure, ideal for sacrificial strangulation. A pleasure to kiss while still warm.

I'm sure every luxury had been lavished on that youth—breast feeding, circumcision, microscopes, scuba diving... Life expectancy was his one weak point. Someone, somewhere, would systematically make him disappear.

When he drop-kicked the empty cider can into the Serpentine I felt my face tighten. Used to be a nice boy, not any more. Dizzy queenling.

From the depths of his baggy cut-offs came a pack of Silk Cut. He smoked half a cigarette standing at the water's edge with his back to me, pretending to have a serious think, tapping the ash more often than necessary. His buttocks were lifted and separated just the way I like them. But it was the shiny declivities behind his lightly tanned hairless knees which I zoomed in on, pale and smooth and obviously soft. Soft as the small of his back or the nape of his neck or the sides of his teenage chest, but not as soft as his insides.

Returning to sit alongside me, knees touching, he continued stubbing out his cigarette on the bench between his legs long after it was extinguished, flinging the stub into the water, hitting the same spot my phlegm had splashed down earlier. At this second litter crime, worthy of a one hundred pound fine, I wanted a good fairy to drop a serviceable implement of torture into my hand. No fairy made my dream come true. Do they ever?

Being a resourceful sort, I speedily improvised. In my head I hoisted his battered body over my right shoulder with choreographed ease, carrying it down to the water's edge, lowering it carefully (arms flopping), maybe even saying something soothing while tugging the clothes off and wiping down the movable parts: stage directions to an intoxicating ritual. (The younger the body, the lighter it is. Convenient for disposal.)

Pulling him by the ankles would have grazed his back, spoiling it. *Carrying* the shipwrecked, washed-up body to the bench, laying the pale flesh down, so passive, so controlled, cleansed and sublimely at peace in the last of the daylight, pale, so pale—practically porcelain. Smooth rose-petal skin stretched over those shapely legs, my fingers running over the surface like braille. Wet, he looked like polished stone. Kneeling in reverence, I was half annoyed that it had all been so fast, I'd missed out monitoring those dying, dimming eyes.

The cider made me burp one of those silent baby burps.

A medium-sized kitchen knife is an unusual item in a puncture repair kit, handy though. I emasculated him with one simple cut, stuffing his church-candle white prick-teasing dick up his arse, a long way up. A coroner would later note that inside the Reebok socks stuffed down the boy's throat, a long way down, were his nipples, sliced off immediately after emasculation. You cannot hurt a corpse.

Perhaps a muscle man with good gripping fingernails could, clutching a buttock in each hand, have ripped the arse then body apart like they do the yellow pages on tv. Imagine that parting of the flesh. Great telly. And this muscle man could say, in a voice close to yodelling, "You'll have no more troubles now, squire" like a *Lassie* film hero giving a helping hand in some dark valley.

When he asked what my flat was like I was thinking that his beautiful empty head would make a cute addition to the Peter Pan statue, mounted sideways on the flute. How children's book sections would swell after the tabloid fuss, with readers searching out the Barry book.

I added three to the last digit when giving him my number.

I had to get real, had to resist. Hands off. *Jailbait.* And not worth it. He said he'd phone me later, from his bed. He said this smiling, as the dropped cigarette was caught on an undercurrent and gently pulled under. Then he winked. I just smiled back saying, "Do that."

It was too dark to wear my glasses as I took the cycle route beneath the stretch of trees towards Speakers Corner, passing the barracks ever so slowly. I realised I was drunk on one can of cider. I'd hardly had a thing to eat all day. Not like me at all.

While Allan was getting a wrong number, I was playing Minor, Seventh and Minor-Seventh chords in the SINGLE FINGER mode (Cm-C7-Cm7), forgetting about myself for a while, lost in the easy manipulations.

Like a fool, I was up and waiting for the postman. I was sitting naked on the sofa, watching breakfast tv with the sound down low, listening out for the familiar flap of the letter-box. I'd been frustrated by the lack of mail at eight thirty, wondering if he had been delayed by the rain. Before deciding to make some tea and watch telly for a bit, I just stood there, staring at the letter-box, then peeping through the spyhole.

A tv presenter I didn't like the look of was reeling off percentages with a smile on her made-up face.

"*...and another survey of four hundred lesbian and gay teenagers revealed that thirty eight per cent felt isolated, thirty two per cent had been verbally abused, nineteen percent had been physically abused and...*"

I gave the presenter a good middle finger when I heard the heavy plain brown envelope finally drop, switching the BBC bitch to a blank screen.

More mail, more dreams. My fascination with stationery and handwriting had gone. I just wanted to see those pictures and feel the longing.

Hi!/Hi there/Wow!/Sir/Dear Sir/Master/Dear....../Dear Whoever/You're the answer to a cocksucker's dream/Bike Boy/Dear Bike Boy/HI MATE!/Dear Boyz advertiser/Good Morning/*TRY THIS FELLA!*/Feeling horny?/I hope you're not a time waster...

I skimmed through the letters like someone conducting market research. The repetition of desire was boring. I had no compassion for these people playing the contact game. My personality had evaporated, had been filed away incorrectly or mislaid for a while. I didn't feel like me.

Seven floors down a line of grey-haired company types in navy blue business suits walked along the Goswell Road like schoolchildren in a crocodile.

Thursday again.

I'd lost interest in the Bike Boy replies which pumped my way. The joke wasn't funny any more. I no longer set my alarm to read it all avidly upon arrival. Enclosed photographs were not returned in the stamped addressed envelopes provided, but formed a spreading collage above the kitchen sink. A herd staring forward.

I unboxed some of Ray's things, searching out his smell in the blackwatch tartan of his Aero Star jacket. Going through his old records, a photograph slipped out from between a Kraftwerk and a Joy Division sleeve. A 10x8 of him in a tweed coat with a question mark badge, neither of which I'd ever seen, a not so bad print on fibre paper. Only the coat was in focus. Ray's face was a blur. He must have moved at the last moment. Maybe he'd been shaking his head, not wanting to have his photo taken. Strangely, the background had been carefully cut away, body mounted on white card. Ray, with a fluffy kind of suede-head look. Sexy. (Who took that picture? Where? When?) It was a Ray I'd never met, handsome and full of life. Ray, part pushy bastard with a head full of awkward questions and a pocketful of Rizlas, part slave to the rhythm. Complete opposites—bound to get on. I'd never been aware enough of what I stood to lose. Cock, tongue, the smell of him. His laugh. Not savoured enough. That smell, once all over my body—then only deep in the mattress, his clothes. The paintings he threw together in an hour, the measurements pencilled on the back of picture frames he'd built out of salvaged wood. His cooking. Ray. It was nice when I reached over to touch him and he was there, night after night. Nothing casual. Ray and me. Together.

I put the picture back where I found it.

Unplugging the phone for a week intensified the silence in the flat. I'd eaten the cupboards bare. I faced a mirror for the first time in a long while to shave and make my surfaces presentable to shoppers and staff at Sainsbury's. Unbrushed teeth were starting to fur. I didn't like my hair at all and a shave became the first bath in days and a good hairwash.

Just as I was locking my bike up next to the *Big Issue* man, rain came down in heavy drops from invisible clouds. The weather forecast had said dry with sunny spells.

More than anything else I felt stupid. Behind my placid face was an aching head with hysteric sobs on cue but never released, a matter-of-fact feeling that I was about to implode, bursting blood, splashing the check-out girl.

Back at the flat I opened the morning mail. Faces smiled up at me from photographs in parks, bedrooms, shower units, final days of a trip somewhere sunny. I spread them out over the living-room floor like tarot cards.

My usual cropping of photographs for the sick joke collage growing like a mould above my kitchen sink turned into a hacking mutilation for one young man named Ben. His chest, pectorals, waist and thighs were perfect—I cut off his ugly head in a snip, mid neck. Hairy forearms were chopped off at the elbows, legs just above the knees. I ate dull flowers of popcorn, getting very hard.

Coming into an ankle sock I realised my hair could do with more than a wash and dab of gel. I needed another haircut, something closer to the scalp. I turned up at Rox, without an appointment. Shaun gave me a variety of smiles and a number two at the back and sides, leaving the top only inches long, gelled tilting forward at a precipitous angle. I

looked like your average London faggot. (Wahey!) The
haircut drew attention away from my eyes, vulnerable to
detection in the cleanshaven mask.

Before opening the envelope, brown and plain as ever, I
stared and stared at a scribble which went round and round
in a big blue loop over the second-class stamp. I wondered
who'd put it there, what significance it might hold. Opening
the envelope I lazily wondered what the people I went to
school with had ended up doing. What had become of those
boys I was crushed alongside in organised, memorised rows?
Philip Blackmore, Dennis Burke, Christopher George.

Counting the envelopes, only nine, totalling up in my
head, fifty eight replies, I thought of my polyester postman.
I'd come to recognise the sound of his feet catching grit with
a lazy shuffle, the dragging gait he'd probably been chastised
for as a child. I resolved to bleach both lift and stairs in
silent thanks for his deliveries which had brought a break
from being me. Once I did jury service at the Old Bailey, on
a rape case for two days. The incident had occurred on a
staircase just like mine. Her screams had gone unheard.

No photos that week, so I added the blue biro looped
stamp to the bottom right of the collage, like a giant full
stop. Looking at the collage I realised I'd forgotten all their
names, their normal names. Names you'd hear paged at an
airport, names which sign school reports, names of
husbands and missing sons. Maybe one or two figure in
Spotlight or Debrett. Maybe a few that will crop up in a
cellar one day, some rubbish dump or drain, recognisable
only through dental records. I scanned the letters with an
unvarying pulse then binned them.

Kenneth Williams dragged a rare laugh from me,
camping it up on the afternoon film as I sifted through past
Bike Boy replies. Men named Stan, Anthony and Costas
were all tuned in to the same channel. Existers of London,
united by the same pathetic B-movie. Their particulars
entered into my diary I binned the lot, returning to my seat
by the window to watch lights pop on over London as the
sky darkened early.

The day was hot and grey. Windless. The glare in the sky cast no shadows. In the small tree-lined street of desirable residences of six to seven floors lived an obese sissy named Stan, one of the maybes. Towering up beside me as I cycled lazily, these were just the kind of buildings to gladden the hearts of the Royal Family and visitors from abroad. The day I cycled down that respectable street, it had a Sunday lunch stink to it. Well-wiped neo-Georgian windows reflected my brand new false self gliding by. For a moment I really enjoyed the way I was inhabiting my body.

Recognising the confident, rounded shapes of his below the buzzer for flat F, I waited for another door to open, welcoming me in. About to ring the bell a third time, half suspecting a practical joke at my expense, I heard the weight of another Bike Boy enthusiast plonking down the stairs.

My pulse thudded steadily and deeply as I switched into Bike Boy mode. As a Yale catch began to turn, I half-removed my Erasure teeshirt. Holding my stomach in, shoulders back, legs apart, moving from flaccid to semi-erect with the theatrics, my first impressions were ready for delivery when the door opened. Arms raised upwards, armpits and torso exposed, otherwise beheaded.

Through the thin white cotton teeshirt I could see the eyes in his sizeable face paying full attention to the lycra shorts. The silence of concentration made me smile. Then the situation made me start to laugh. The air felt cool when I'd finished my tease, exposing my cheerful-seeming face within a metre of his.

"Beautiful day, isn't it?" my other voice said straight into his eyes, like a regular delivery boy.

Far worse than the greying wild guitar-string hair slipping through his string vest, more horrible than the dyed boomerang moustache and tight little black shorts, were his nipples. Poking through the aforesaid string vest, they resembled those pinky bits you get in uncooked mince meat. They protruded proudly from D-cup breasts with an above average rate of juggleosity; a body guaranteed to empty public swimming pools. An ideal specimen to tick off as another human experience.

CALL ME

"Hell-o," he said. "Come on in. Straight up."

He wanted to watch my arse in motion up the stairs. I ascended in threes. He had to race to keep up floor by floor with the vision of maximum crack.

In the converted attic I smelled nose-bleeds and toffees. Green walls were covered with pictures of fattening years scientifically documented on glossy photographic paper. Narcissism gone mad. Group shots galore taken at Rosh Hashanah, Yom Kippur and a variety of nudist beaches. While he got busy with the kettle, red in the face and panting, I went to the loo, taking my pannier in with me. Lowering the toilet seat I just sat there, eyes drifting from tanning pills to Fruits of the Forest air freshener and Body Shop seaweed-and-pomegranate shampoo. It was nice to be away from the rumble of the Goswell Road. Assorted seashells were scattered by the bath and many new-age crustaceans awaited discovery in the shagpile. The bidet taps seeped; twisting both off at once I detected oil or lubricant on them.

Above and around the well-splashed full-length mirror, pin-up boys from wank mags stared. Others came from teen zines: Take That, Bad Boys Inc and East 17 were all there— prime, pumped, waxed, tanned, moisturised boy-flesh giving their best knowing smiles and very convincing big thick dick looks. I raised a pistol-shaped hand and aimed between my eyes. From the back of my mouth a slow gust of breath hit my teeth, an attempt at a slow-motion bang. My breath steamed the mirror.

I took centre stage in the kitchen as the kettle steamed. I was still only guessing but my guess was that this sissy fairy had been a plump but pretty little poofter at school, always saying the wrong first words. Always planning how to get to school safely, arriving on the bell. Master-minding how to get through break, questioning teachers on the finer details of homework just set, making the librarian feel wanted at lunchtime with fastidious questions and cute vulnerability.

He looked neither cute nor vulnerable during the food orgy. He'd made the scones himself, jam too. Crumpets and muffins came out of wrappings he tried hard to conceal. Cheese, fruit and a tin of butter biscuits awaited incisors, molars and the internal squeeze. He clearly had a tendency to consume far more than he could metabolize.

Chewing in time to the second hand of his very new old fake Rolex, he seemed to be enjoying himself. Fancied a taste of me, too. For half an hour I nodded drowsily to everything he said and he had a lot to say. He obviously read newspapers and the occasional bit of queer theory on Cassell. Long rows of thin-spined paperbacks, lined up by the kitchen window, made interesting head-turned-sideways reading as he droned on about Bosnia, Clinton and the age of consent.

"I don't usually reply to ads, you see. I prefer to be on the receiving end, if you know what I mean."

"Right."

"My interest mainly lies in shorts and..."

"Go on."

"Well, my ad went something like, *Jewish Y-fronts enthusiast WLTM discreet non scene young guy (18-35) wearing white Y-fronts. ALA. London/Anywhere.*"

"*Uncut particularly welcome!*"

"Oh, you've seen it. What a good memory you have. I'll have to watch what I say."

"Not a bad idea."

"Shall we..." he said, standing.

An old record Liza Minelli had made with The Pet Shop Boys was all cued up. *PLAY* was pressed. A short walk away at the other side of the long sitting-room (turquoise pencil-shaving pot pourri ad infinitum) another *PLAY* button was activated with the same index finger. A video featuring Dutch boys in pre-virus action had been carefully selected and lined up to a favourite section. No pre-plague moaning or groaning was to be heard. I sat by the window on a decorative stool between curtains (with heavy emphasis on flounce) that pooled down to form two dusty heaps. It probably wasn't intended for sitting on but it was the furthest seat from him.

"This is nice," I lied, running a hand over carved legs.

"Moroccan. Went there years ago, in search of boys. Well, got so sunburned the first day I couldn't move from the balcony for a week which only left three days for trade, peeling. Should've seen the blisters. My dear! Two boys I 'ad. Got pickpocketed and crabs."

"A frequent combination."

The video, badly transferred, was in shades of cobalt. A boy, probably seventeen, maybe sixteen, fair skin turned blue, strolled out of a blue bathroom with a pale blue towel around his blue neck while unbuckling the big black belt on his torn jeans, ignoring an almost identical (skeletal) blue boy on a blue bed wearing tight blue-white Y-fronts. The boy on the bed began jerking off with a weird sense of loss, acting like the bathroom boy wasn't there. No newcomer to videos, masturbating nice and slowly, getting it right for the cameras. Then the bathroom boy, inexperienced, rushed in, lowering those blue jeans and undies too quickly for the cameras to savour. For Stan the dressed moments were the most erotic though he did his best to look genuinely bored. No inch to pinch on either of them. Nice. There was a bit of kissing, gentle fondling and much made of a bit of blue pre-cum on one of the blue cocks, then the lovely skinny back of the bathroom boy stretched long as he entered the bedroom boy's blue buttocks. I like that area around the kidneys when it's totally fat free, without moles or hair. The boys seemed to share an evenness of inhalation and exhalation.

I bet Stan's thumb had blistered with the picture search of his remote, rewinding, fast forwarding and viewing frame by frame. £20 of VHS, worth every penny. Liza sang, the boys fucked. A dark line of sweat defined the crack of Stan's fat arse as he minced off towards the bathroom. Baggy old arse, arse like a windsock. The only way to treat such an arse is to fuck it hard, making it tighten up, providing an adequate amount of internal friction to get off.

Through the half-closed door I saw him take a leak, shake his cock. He farted loudly and then, like a dog, moved his head a little to sniff. I think he smiled. By the mirror he paused to check the pores of each nostril, then his breath. He was back in the room after the briefest gargle.

Confident as to the state of his nose and breath he walked straight over to me (I thought he was going to open the window) and put his hands around my neck very fast, squeezing deeply but gently. A strange sort of massage. His crotch was at eye-level, horrid and faintly smelly. Hands moved to the top of my shoulders, kneading like a hausfrau. Then he lunged, the horrible mouth on mine, sticky lips glistening like fly-paper spreading up and over mine.

His mouth was very soft and with my eyes closed the feeling transferred into a very dull crimson. The inside of his mouth was too roomy, his sloppy tongue attempting to refill dried-up emotions by licking my front teeth. That same tongue had probably disappeared into arseholes, savouring body juices from paid-for bodies. When he took a step back to assess the situation, I must have flashed an expert vile smile because he popped off back to the bathroom with the air of a thirteen-year-old playing Cleopatra, shutting the door behind him with the hint of a bang, all feelings concentrated upon that which is detached, outwards and outgoing—his sunrise circumcised winkle.

His diary, stupidly left beside the phone, went into my pannier beside a knife taken from the magnetic frame. If I'd known he was going to get the Accu-Jac kit out I'd have pinched a paperback or two or made for his CD collection.

I listened at the door. All was quiet. I imagined him at the mirror brandishing a small but tremendously thick purple-headed erection, wanked to excess in pre-obese teenage years. A dick which had helped him forget the distress of days alone, brightened with jerking off in tree-houses, basements, attics, toilets. I could almost smell the sweet counterfeit orgasm, the swimming-pool chlorine, locker rooms of rugby boy smell and those dreaded showers.

I heard his 'aah' steaming up the looking glass in that final moment behind the bathroom door, the room becoming an echo chamber for just a moment. In the dark he'd been called beautiful. In the dark he'd been loved.

When he came out I was merely the relic of a mood to be shot of asap. I declined his offer of one last cup of tea. The weather had changed. It had turned out to be another boiling hot day.

Fat Man Stan's diary got splashed in the bath but that

didn't matter. He had nothing special to say either to me or his diary. Royal blue ink stained the water as the diary submerged.

Dreary day, tiring day.

I sent Costas a DIY Polaroid, sealing down a recycled first class stamp with a smile. I didn't give my number or anything, just wrote, in capital letters:

WILL PHONE SOON—BIKE BOY.

This was executed with a black biro, pressing hard.

I'd phoned him up and he sounded worth investigation. A photo was his one stipulation. He got what he asked for. He sounded different. A different type. Somewhere between innocent, naive and stupid. Sexy.

Shortly after I arrived, rain fell suddenly against the perspex skylight with the uneven sound of a cheap shower. The place was furnished with junk shop finds. Taste not dissimilar to Ray's. Functional, thirties. He'd got me reclining in a beaten-up armchair, highly contentious Michael Jackson teeshirt draped around my shoulders. Ludicrous. Everything was quite pleasant in the garden flat and the erection in my lycra shorts was as evident as his in denim.

After maybe half an hour the rain stopped. We'd both got used to having a sound backdrop. Putting down a pencil, he pressed *PLAY* and Duke Ellington came to life for what felt like a to-the-minute scheduled break from the sketching.

Charles from Brockley made a fine cup of tea and never got to finish his sketch. A not-bad-at-all kiss led on to a pretty fast blowjob in the kitchen. The kiss was a matter of lips and tongues meeting. No warmth, no tenderness— purely physical. With my eyes closed I found myself comparing his kissing technique with Ray's. He liked to be on the receiving end of a tongue.

After the kiss he was down on his knees, a position I supposed he frequently took with his occasional models. In a somewhat routine manner jeans and shorts were lowered, then he got busy throating. I didn't tell him I was about to come which brought a smile to his face and a groan through his chest as I did. "Mmm," he went as he pebble-dashed the cork tiles with his load. Although I'd estimate that on the Wechler intelligence scale Charles would score a full IQ of one hundred and eighteen, placing him in the bright normal category, he swallowed. He was okay. He was the kind you could have sleepy Sundays with, the kind who'd iron a shirt for you. Good with mothers.

One question led to another. A photographer? Who have you worked for? So why have you jacked it all in?

"I haven't jacked it all in, as you put it. I'm just taking a break. I could go out and knock off a nightclub feature tomorrow. Anyone can cobble together a bit of copy on some dragged up DJ in her thirties playing records at six in the morning. Some new Steve Strange/Leigh Bowery trash bash door whore, drag king, whatever, but what's it worth? I've been looking over my laminates lately. I wasn't put on this Earth to document street-style for the likes of *An-An*."

"*An-An?*"

"It's a Jap magazine. A lot of what I do goes abroad."

"Standing back from it all for a while then, yes?"

"Basically, basically I'm fed up with it all. I could go into teaching, I've got the qualifications."

"The world is your oyster." He sounded patronising but wasn't. If the doorbell hadn't rung, I might have stayed the night. Unexpected Sunday guests fresh from shopping at Camden Lock walked straight on in demanding coffees. Unexpected, uninvited and unwelcome.

I sat for a polite period, feeling the stubble bristling on my arms before going, saying I'd phone at seven. He was one of the few people I thought I'd bother with again. Bit social worker, though.

At seven I was in the bath, shaving all over, humming the national anthem—Ray's old winceyette pyjamas waiting for me.

Yet another beautiful sunset, making me sad. The more beautiful the skies, the uglier the rooftops. A school nurse once said: "If you're feeling sad, hum to yourself, it'll help." Depends what you hum.

I never really understood the mysteries of the INTRO/FILL IN button, used in the Auto Accompaniment mode to create pattern variations. When this button was held down, the FILL IN pattern was supposed to repeat until released, then the normal rhythm would start from the beginning of the next measure. I think.

When I sat behind the keyboards I usually focused on a spot far off, a vanishing point somewhere, often unaware of changes in light or temperature, recording the same piece over and over again until it felt right. I had nearly fifty cassettes of the stuff. Sometimes that vanishing point was a body at the bus stop, sometimes the moon.

From the light blue, stone-washed jeans to the perm—gold flashing, very Greek—he was a *Daily Mirror* reader. He was different from the rest but he too needed to talk. The flat was like a storage warehouse, stacked with goodies for his future dream home.

"She's not my big love or anything, she's just going to have my baby, 'bout eight weeks from now."

"And you've also got a girlfriend at the moment."

"Oh yeah, but she's just, you know, just a girl. You know. I won't marry her. Wouldn't dream of it. Good for now, that's all. I want to marry a virgin girl. My parents will choose someone nice. You see, the way I look at it is gay men don't stick together long an' what I want is forever. Must be. I couldn't stand the pain of getting it all together then watching it fall apart. I don't want to go an' tell me parents that I'm in love with some guy an' we're an item an' that, right? Then he goes off with some bloke down Brief Encounter or Kudos an' that's it. Over. No way."

He took a sip of his Pepsi.

"I'd like a big man, a real hunk. Just us two...but it ain't gonna happen, right? Cos it jus' don't in this world, right? You know what I mean. You know. You know I'm right. I can mess around before I marry but won't when I am."

The book club had done very nicely out of Mr Costas Bourboulous. He'd got a bit of everything for his future family.

"So, cos you didn't have nice books and nice furniture

when you were a kid, you've been collecting all this for when you get married, for your *ideal home* as you put it?"

He was smiles all of a sudden.

"Yeah, that's my dream."

"And you really haven't even looked at any of these books yourself?" I said, replacing a two pound weight of glossy Van Gogh on the shelf weighed down with taste.

"No, you see, I'm not educated. It's too late for me. But I want my children to be educated, see?"

"And you go to saunas, discos, bars...in the hope of meeting Mr Right."

"Yeah. An' I have a lot of fun too. Down York Hall in Bethnal Green, Starsteam in Battersea, 309 in New Cross, very handy, and Pacific 33 up Holloway. Perspiration in King's Cross was good, got busted though. Sub Station's my favourite club at the moment, I'm tired of Heaven. But all I get is a wank, a blow job or two. Hardly very romantic. There are a lot who are right, but gay men just don't stick together. There's always temptation. Queers just ain't faithful. I'll have a wife in a few years. I'll be out of this place and have somewhere nice and respectable. My own."

Over by the window the British Home Stores' watering instructions had been ignored. The pretty things were scorched. Waiting to be disposed of, replaced. Seventeen floors below, I saw him again. The boy from half an hour back.

Arriving too early I'd sat myself down on a bench by the river, just watching the boats go by. He must have been a dangerous fourteen. Too tall for his age, blond with an outgrowing flat-top. Dressed in a baggy black and blue check shirt and jeans, hole at the knee. A Deanager, brimming with pubescent essence. The shirt, printed not woven, was open, drawing attention to nipples like faint stains under the white cotton of his vest, radiating sexuality. An un-fucking-believable looking kid, mouth-watering. The tightest pores. It wouldn't be long before those teenage looks would be all dried up, his skin crying out for liposomes.

I was wearing a naff LONDON teeshirt. No illustrations, just bold block capitals in half a dozen colours.

L-O-N-D-O-N. Tourist crap. That's what I thought he was smiling at to start with. Then I thought it was the bike. He sat right next to me. There in the open, illegally close. The close proximity of the boy alone felt like a highly punishable offence. He turned his face towards me slowly and gave a perfect smile. (As he exhaled I didn't waste the opportunity to fill my own lungs.) The single, steel, horizontal line across his upper teeth drew me like a magnet. I had to rock away a bit on my buttocks to form a suitable gap between our knees. He whistled a single which had gone straight into the charts that week at number five. I liked the tune, had rewatched the 'Chart Show' video several times, but couldn't remember who it was by.

The policeman inside my head moved me along. I had no idea where I was going, just away from him. Timewasting. He followed.

Under a block of flats he moved ahead, then turned. It was dark there with smelly recesses people wouldn't want to slip and fall into. Looking down at his trainers, both laces undone, his eyes changed angle slowly, gliding across wet concrete, up and over my body, arriving at my eyes fixed on his. It was the kind of darkness your vision soon adjusts to and so conveniently quiet you could hear anyone approaching even from quite a distance. Enough time to pull your shorts or torn jeans up and move on out like you'd only been mending a puncture or something.

His hands were plunged deep into his 501s, head tilted back a little. Full frontal come on, come and get me. Belt undone, buckle dangling, young pelvis thrust forward, crotch contours clearly visible and excitingly impressive. A body (his mother had once sworn) made for sex. He was desperate to break open the promising package of his teens.

His body language whispered to me: "I've a calling. I'm every faggot's cute kid brother, the one they all wished they'd had to abuse." Had he parted his lickable, bee-stung lips, that's what he would have said.

He took a step closer to me as I took two in his direction. I've heard that the dark line above a teenage boy's lip is a lovely, very special texture to tongue, so long as that

CALL ME

teenager hasn't had his first shave. I could have had him there, by the bins, leaving him young, dumb and full of cum. Just one minute with a kid so fresh to puberty could mean years in Whitemoor or some such place. (*Who knows who you could meet?*) Maybe he could sense I had a condom in my wallet, beside a beautifully sharpened knife.

I didn't see the look on his face as I got on my bike, but his wolf-whistle sounded like he was smiling. Yes, it was the same boy, seventeen floors down, below, circling the main entrance of Costas' building on his racer. At nine, ten, maybe up to thirteen, I'd been dangerous like that: looking for a kiss. Hanging around parks, swimming pools, the edges of a golf course—wanting contact. Didn't get it.

"See something you like?" Costas asked.

We both watched the boy on the bike below while sipping the strongest tea ever from the best of Petticoat Lane rejects. British Rail variety, far too strong. Shelves of china animals and little ladies with parasols sat collecting dust, waiting for a beautiful home and a beautiful wife.

He wanted action by the time he'd finished his cuppa. He wanted a dick in his gob. He wanted to have his circumcised cock handled the way no woman he'd yet met could. And so did that boy.

Jessie Scott from next door, a strong and friendly woman, was the only neighbour I ever got talking to. She knocked four solid raps soon after I moved in with Ray to ooh and aah the bleaching of the stairs and lift which I did with keen regularity for my first two years there. These oohs and ahhs were delivered in an accent with strong Buchan roots. She caught me crying on the staircase once, having difficulty with the keys, and gave me a hug.

She was from Fraserburgh, Aberdeenshire, and proud of it. Her introduction followed the usual formality, the offer of half a cup of sugar or pint of milk should the need arise.

Her flat was hot and heavy with the smell of roasts and boiled veg. Pride of place went to a large china cocker spaniel with *TaRzaN* Tipp-Exed at the base. It supposedly resembled a treasured pet, long since gone. Put down. Tears had been shed. She had a son she hadn't seen in a long while and never said much about. Never said a word about the father and a certain forcefield kept questions at bay.

"Now Liam," she launched off, "I wonder if you'd do me a favour. That brother of mine has taken another fall and I'm going to have to go up to visit him in hospital this time. Would you look after Hamish for a while?"

Hamish was a depressed-looking budgerigar, frozen to his perch. Tiny. Green with a yellow head, blue above the beak. A male. *HaMiSh* was written in more Tipp-Ex on the frame of his cage. He shivered when Jessie's face approached to ask if he were a good, pretty little boy. The bird was shrinking with age, but unlike Jessie had no surplus flesh on the bones to draw from.

"Now, you don't have to change the water every day if you don't want to. Every few days will do. He likes lettuce or a bit of cabbage. Here's a few copies of *The News Of The World* for his tray. I don't go in for sandpaper, too pricey and makes a mess. I like to think he likes the pictures."

The creature with a brain the size of a split pea looked up, embarrassed at having his shitting needs made so public.

"Right. Now, if you need to put your hand in then watch out, he'll peck. He's a real little nipper. Fast as fast and he'll be out in a flash, flying into windows and mirrors."

Hamish looked stupid amongst his rattling swing, mirror and balls. His eyes were black dots except when excited or saying the only words he knew in Jessie's voice: "Piss off!"

"And you *will* need to put your hand in. His mirror is important cos he thinks it's another budgie. Needs to be cleaned each day, if you don't mind."

In a plastic bag passed over the threshold that Jessie had never crossed were rations of millet seed, a whole iceberg lettuce, four apples, a cuttlefish and a vitamin block he would not need. There was also a very large chocolate bar and a thankyou card—for me.

"Don't let him out, he'll dirty everywhere and eat your earlobes off. He's quite happy with his ladder and mirror."

Hamish twittered neurotically at first, but he soon

settled down. When he sat on my shoulders, stretching forward to natter in my ear, I could feel the innocent warmth of his chest on my cheek, also smelling of age and fragility.

It had been a long while since there'd been singing in the flat. Ray used to hold me in his arms and sing to me.

ABUSER
FRIENDLY

Stalking the pages became my very own alternative to tv. I bought every publication running contact ads I could find. Besides the obvious choices (*Time Out, Sky, Gay Times* and *Dateline*), I bought *Loot, The Spectator, Melody Maker, NME, Private Eye, What's On In London, Him, Gay Scotland* plus the soon to be defunct *Phase* and *Bona.*

Then there were the freebies like *Capital Gay, The Pink Paper, Link Up, All Points North, Gay Community News* and *Guyz*, available in bars and clubs. I didn't reply to ads in *Boyz*, not even at the discount rate of four for a fiver. Most of the publications wanted a couple of first-class stamps enclosed per reply. *Sky* was the odd one out, with a Freepost service as an incentive. I was drawn to the odd, the pathetic and bizarre. Easy catches. I replied to ads across the sexual spectrum.

In the back of *The London Weekly Advertiser* I spotted an ad: 'Contacts On Video, The essential new contact service. See your contacts first, LIVE ON VIDEO!!!'

I sent off a cheque for fifteen pounds, hoping to see the couples seeking single girls, couples seeking single men, couples seeking couples, mature women (40+) seeking men, voyeurs seeking couples, housewives seeking single men (husband present), TV/TS seeking straight guys, all on home-made videos with sound, but nothing arrived. I felt hugely disappointed and wrote a letter of complaint to a south London address.

I replied to about forty ads, sending the more tasteful free postcards available in Village. Over and over I wrote the same brief reply in royal blue ink, using an italic nib specially purchased for the job. Top right I wrote the full date, beneath which sat my phone number. Slap bang in the middle went the fake name in capital letters. Below this, in neat cursive, I wrote: *Call me.* (Even if the ad begged a photo or frank letter this is all they got.) Bottom right went the socially dishonest signature, using cheerful and safe rounded shapes. I like to think it all looked more discreet than devious. Recycled stamps were Pritt Sticked down to thick, white Conqueror envelopes. I delivered my replies to the various offices around town on my bike after dark.

Choosing fake names for myself became an alphabetic chore, more time and effort went into matching a name to an ad than the random selection of victim. Within seconds of a call for, say, Matthew, I'd know the ad had been in *Dateline* reading:

> **I WANT an aristocratic** English young man—6' tall, slim...a bit like Sting but ideally dark. I'm 29, female, like tennis, badminton, choir, folk singing. Smart businessman for very special friendship with same interests.

On the wall by the phone my little list awaited calls. Instant recall gave a ring of sincerity, as though theirs was the only ad I'd responded to. Every time that phone rang Hamish leapt from perch to perch, ringing his bell, pecking at his mirror as if in on the game.

Aaron   **Time Out**
SEXY PRETTY WOMAN, 42, likes music, cinema, theatre, seeks attractive younger man for going out, staying in, affection and fun fun fun. Photo/phone appreciated.

(*Affection* is more likely to mean infection.)

Brian   **Sky**
TRANSVESTITE, 28. Average height, fashionable, WLTM sincere, understanding, professional male, 18-35, as friend/escort to drag balls, nightclubs etc. Discretion assured. Long letter receives same. Afternoons free.

Cerith *Gay Community News*
ATTRACTIVE YOUNG GAY GUY seeks special quiet friend (18+) to share my life with. I live quietly in my secluded home in Brighton near coast. I am totally loyal, caring, loving, non-scene, rather lonely and you will not be disappointed by my looks or personality. ALAWP.

(*Attractive* means not. A well-known, tiresome fact.
Afternoons free, the appointed fucking hour.)

Daniel   *Time Out*

CAUTION! DEADLY SERIOUS ADVERTISEMENT!
PLEASE STUDY CAREFULLY BEFORE REPLYING.

You could be aged anywhere between 18 and 24. 6`, clean-shaven and poised between simple college boyishness and bronzed muscular Adonis. You're the sort "they" call a "hunk". Your eyes are bluest blue, your hair fair to mid-brown, your smile sparkling. The quintessential model of desirable masculinity and what's more, you know it. This morning, as always, you spent two hours in the gym. "They" say it's an obsession but to you it's a way of life. You enjoy the effect on others—the admiring glances, the way heads turn when you walk into a room. Some day your face and body will make your fortune—that's for sure. But right now you lack direction—that's where I come in. At 32 years of age, I am a businessman who has gained success and recognition in a highly competitive sector of the entertainment industry and I am looking for a young guy EXACTLY like YOU to share my expensive, exciting life-style. Why deprive yourself of the finer things in life—good food, luxurious surroundings, prestige cars, world travel—when I can realise your ambitions. Pale imitations beware. This golden opportunity is reserved EXCLUSIVELY for the ONE guy portrayed above. He knows who he is, so will I. Send me your photo NOW and let's talk.

Euan   **Capital Gay**
STRUT IT! Exhibitionists, strippers, DIY fans sought by South London guy. 33, tall, slim, own place, videos. Tea and cake after! Photo/Phone helps.

Gary   **Loot**
GILLIAN, TRANSVESTITE. 28. Bored! Seeking young man for friendship and fun. Into TIGHT skirts, high heels, squeezable rears. Long letter please.

(Bored means boring.)

Frank   **Time Out**
GLAMOUROUS TRANSVESTITE, 26, seeks tall, attractive, masculine, guy for fun times. (18+) Frank letter appreciated.

Horst   **Loot**
ATTRACTIVE CONTINENTAL WLTM intelligent guy or couple for lustful (safe) erotic adventures. Photo + frank letter please.

(Continental, an Arab?)

Ian What's On In London
JULIET LONGS FOR ROMEO but will settle for bright, debonair, film/theatre-loving man, 25-35. Photo, letter appreciated but humour/integrity essential.

(Use of the word *debonair,* a sure sign of awful taste.)

Jon The Pink Paper
ATTRACTIVE GUY, 38, smart, businessman, straight lifestyle. Seeking clean-cut professional for discreet, safe friendship. ALA. Photo helpful. (Returned.)

(*Discreet,* marriage wrecker)

Kieran Gay Times
SATIN FETISH GUY, 32, attractive, slim, muscular, WLTM satin clad guys, 18-35, for safe smooth fun. ALA. Phone. Photo.

Luke Capital Gay
RECENTLY INTO LEATHER. 40. London search on for younger guy needing strict training. Meet soon, my place. Possible 1-2-1?

Marc The Pink Paper
ROCKABILLY BOY, 22, straight-acting, inexperienced, DA! Seeks similar guy, 18-28 for very special friendship with same interests.

(*Same interests*—see *bored.*)

L is for *loves to cuddle*...mediocre fuck.
M—*Model*...may charge.
N—*Non-camp*...uptight around camp boys.
O—*Occasionally moody*... suicidal tendencies.
P—*Professional*...may pay.
Q—*Quiet*...quite hard work.
R—*Radical*...out to lunch in 501s.

Neil Sky
MARRIED MAN (30) WLTM young London guy with own flat for lunchtime fun. The wife need never know. I'm a generous professional, attractive, discreet with a lot to give the right young guy. (I'm used to being the husband.) 18-24 preferred.

Owen The Pink Paper
WELSH CHAP, 39, lives two hours from London. Soon to start visiting London every Wednesday for a year on a course. Searching for nice lad to meet up with after the long day. Dinner on me! Please write. Genuine. No timewasters please.

Patrick Time Out
SENSITIVE WOMAN, 29, seeks young gay guy, (18+), for friendship.

(I don't know why but I gave this sensitive woman

my address as well as my phone number.)

JF Quinn   **Capital Gay**
ELEGANT BERKSHIRE DAD, 50, WLTM smart son, late teens/early twenties, who also wants a loving, monogamous relationship.

CALL ME

Roger   **Capital Gay**
MATURE MASCULINE GUY seeks one-legged guys. Amputees only. Write to Harry. London/Anywhere.

Sid   **Gay Times**
LONDON SCHOOLMASTER. Handsome. Good body. Strict. Clean-shaven. Well versed in schoolroom manner. 34. Seeking new pupils willing to learn. Good looking? Aged between 18 and 24? OTK CP? Apply! Emphasis on discretion and health at all times. Prefects welcome.

Timothy   **Guyz**
CARING BLACK MALE, 25, 6` 2``, into fitness, music, uninterested in gay scene. WLTM healthy, VWE white boy, non-smoker, non-drinker, similar age and interests, for big fun.

Uri   **NME**
CREATIVE AMERICAN FEMALE seeks LONDON friends. Arriving soon. PO Box 342, Pittsburgh, USA.

(I sent off a pretty impressive letter all about London's wild and wicked clubland. Instantly regretted on posting.)

Viktor   **Him**
BRIAN (RECENTLY 18), little lost lamb, WLTM big daddy sheep (25+) for various ramifications. One man and his dog preferred. Staff supplied. Baaaaa!

William   **Capital Gay**
PINSTRIPE ANARCHIST, gay male, 34. Science-fiction fan, seeks punk guy or similar for fun evenings enjoying a drink or two and watching videos. Fancy something different?

(S—*Science-fiction*...acid tab tendencies. See *bored*.)

Ziggy   **NME**
JAPANESE FEMALE: Likes Primal Scream, U2, Blur, R.E.M., Bjork, Momus, Kate Bush, Enya, Joy Division, Depeche Mode etc. Dislikes: boy bands, Benetton, gym bods. Wants any friends for fun in London. Write to Keiko at —, —— Rd, London, W3 8QJ.

I steered clear of those who compared themselves to vintage cars, historic or cartoon characters. Avoided any who mentioned teddy bears. Turned a blind eye on those who described themselves as vivacious, zany, cultured, into pyjamas/uniforms/socks/pierced nipples—rejected the writer unpublished as yet and the life and soul of many a party... someone into balloons.

In 1876 Alexander Graham Bell discovered that when one metal reed at the end of a line vibrated another at the opposite end, a sound was produced. This was patented as the first practical telephone. This wondrous invention can also be used as an instrument of terror.

"Hello, is Aaron there?"

She phoned four times. We spoke for forty five minutes, thirty five minutes, fifteen minutes and ten. *Time Out* Box number V903. The first of the callers, top of the list.

"Yes, speaking."

"Um, you wrote to me. Answered my ad. One of many probably." A delicate little telephone voice, trembling.

"No, only yours. So you're the 'Sexy Pretty Woman, 42' who likes music and theatre seeking..."

"Gosh. I'm impressed. Wow! You've got a great memory! It's very embarrassing actually. I didn't know how to attract attention and that's why it really, um, came out like that. Probably sounds dreadful, but it's not meant to."

She gave a nervous little laugh then got serious with her spiel. As the conversation progressed the incendiary glow reflected in the clouds became, little by little, fainter. "Anyway, I work in an art gallery handling admin, wha do you do?"

"I take photographs for fashion and music magazines. Youth culture stuff, nothing too fancy though."

"Working in fashion you must meet a lot of people. All those models, you're spoiled for choice really!"

She laughed that little laugh again.

"Bet you got a big response with your ad," I said.

"Oh, it's so embarrassing, yes. The postman had to ring. Couldn't get the bag, the...um...couldn't get the...er..."

"Plain brown envelope?"

"Yes! Couldn't get the envelope through the door...through the letter-box."

"Fan mail!"

She gave a little giggle with delicate breaths.

"It was only when I sent it off that I thought, my God! What have I done? I'd described myself so, well...I'm not sure if I can live up to people's fantasies of this sexy pretty woman. After all, beauty is in the eye of the beholder."

She was one of those people you start counting with, totting up every *so, well, um* and *er* in your head.

"I just wanted to see what...I just wanted to grab attention and go from there. To at least get noticed. I had some nice letters and one of them was yours."

The postcard I'd sent was too brief to be "nice". The demand to call was curt, if anything.

"I don't know if you have a particular sort of, er, build or style in mind but..." her voice went suddenly sad and pathetic and small. Petite. "I'm about five foot three, I suppose, and my hair's dark brown, shortish at the moment, um, and I'm a sort of slim average build."

The clouds paled, became opalescent and slowly dissipated.

"That's what I look like," said like she half expected the phone down on her. She continued in a hoarse whisper, "All I was saying, all I was really trying to get over in the ad was—I was still alive. Hello...I'm still alive. Anyway, you sound nice. What is, you know, I've said my height and...can you give me, er, a picture of yourself?"

"Six foot, slim, short dark hair, smart appearance. Public School education, own teeth, twenty four."

"Oh! You *are* young! So, what do you, um, what sort of things do you wear? Are you casual, jeans and, you know, or...how do you, what's..."

"I'm aware of fashion but not a slave to it. Smart and classic but relaxed, too. Fun without being a clown." It was the sort of stuffiness she wanted to hear and I gave it to her in my best hetero tone of voice. "Suits mainly," I added.

"Oh. Right. Yes. Lovely. So, suits rather than jeans and

leather jackets. If you're tall you can carry a suit."

I sat on the kitchen floor in baggy old Y-fronts ready for the bin and a Seditionaries tits teeshirt, looking at the distant, solitary, fading sun. She hit me with some bull about how she'd love to meet up but it was so hectic for the next week. Could she call back to fix up a time and place? I knew she'd be a phone case. After twenty five minutes of polite and very boring ping-pong chit-chat, I asked my first and only question of the 'Sexy Pretty Woman, 42'.

"What's your name?"

"Oh, sorry. Did I not say? I'm Anne, with an *E*."

"With an E."

"With an *E*, yes. Like the royal Anne."

Maybe she just took a lot of getting to know. In her second call she procrastinated a full fifteen minutes about where to meet, bearing in mind the weather and the problem of recognising each other. She postponed the arrangement in her third call. While Hamish clambered up and down the telephone line and I watched *Top Of The Pops* with the sound down, she said a lot about nothing. I think she thought I was a good listener.

I imagine she goes home to a Sainsbury's fresh free range boiled egg (size 2, class A), takes interesting holidays out of season with a dull, secure companion. Poor Anne with an *E*. Nine to five and 0.5 alive. She said it herself in her last call:

"You drift through childhood, go to school, suddenly it hits you that unless you're very wealthy or a tremendous entrepreneur, um, you know...to actually keep yourself alive, let alone anything else, you have actually got to sell your time. Right? And that's it then. How many people do the things they like? Hence the appeal of holidays."

Anne with an *E*, stuck in bread and butter land. We never met.

"JF Quinn Esquire?" His voice was nasal and camp, slightly northern. Bolton, perhaps.

"Yes, speaking."

"Hi, um, well...this must be the shortest note I've ever had off anyone. I was very intrigued. You obviously don't like to commit yourself in a letter, but then again, your presentation said a lot. Nicely laid out, I'll give you that. Loved the signature and oh, the name...what should I call you? Can't go calling you JF Quinn now, can I?"

"John. John Francis, after my grandfather."

"And I'm Graeme, that's G-R-A-E-M-E, not G-R-A-H-A-M. I was fifty two weeks ago."

"Did you have a good one?"

"Thank you, yes. Wonderful. Can't believe I've actually, actually reached it. Um...er...and how old are you John?"

"Twenty two."

"God, I'm over twice your age! It's very strange, John, but since I got past forty five I seem to meet people who like older men. And I'm surprised, quite honestly, cos I never did, you know. It's wonderful. Wonderful. Yes. It's terrific. Um, what else...anything you want to know about me?"

"Tell me all."

"Okay then. I go to a gym three times a week. I like to look after what I've got and I've got a forty inch chest, twenty nine inch waist. Um, I don't know if you'd think this a plus or a minus but I'm bald. I don't know how you feel about that, whether it bothers you or what."

"Great, specially if it shines."

"It shines!"

"Great!"

Chinese hold that of ten bald men, nine are deceitful, the tenth dumb.

"And I think the ad read 'Elegant City Gent'. I'm very much into, um, formal dress. I find it, well, it quite turns me on actually. Suits, stiff collars, the whole shebang. And the younger people I've met also like it. I don't know if you're looking for a father figure but it...well...they don't like to see older men dressed in jeans. Actually I'm in jeans at the moment but only occasionally for casual, you know. When I go to work...I run a stationery shop, not mine, run it for a friend, straight friend. I've run it for the last twenty two years. Quite tatty actually. Near Liverpool Street."

"In fact your ad read 'Elegant Berkshire Dad', the one I replied to anyway."

"Oh, that one. I didn't realise that one was out yet. I've got a few on the boil right now. Ah, that is interesting. Oh, by the way, I do have all my own teeth. Every one of them. I'm a bit fanatical about that actually. Check-ups every three months. I don't take sugar but do keep it in the house for guests. But apart from that, John, I have all the usual vices. Oh, I gave up smoking three years ago. So, um, well...you know, that's me. Do you wear suits?"

"Yes."

"You do? Ah! Do you like the formal look?"

"I've always been one to polish my shoes."

"I'm very glad. You know, probably because I was in the army for three years, I cannot stand to see a nice suit and scruffy shoes. Drives me mad. I polish my shoes every night so they're ready for the morning. It can all get a bit pricey. Do you know how much it costs to have my collars cleaned and starched? Two pounds twenty, each!"

"I used to get mine from Denny's in Old Compton Street. Wing collars."

He got very excited very quickly. His breathing seemed to stutter, he was gagging.

"Oh! You actually wear them!"

"Not now. It was just a phase I was going through."

"Did they turn you on? Wearing them, you know. Being out in them."

"I liked the way they altered my posture. The stiffness around the neck. Heads turned as I made an entrance, usually with a group of lads from university out for the night somewhere, knocking back bottles of champagne at Kettners or some such place."

"Wonderful. I mean, I never dreamed when you answered my ad that you would like them as well. In fact I've had to explain to a few what they are. My favourites are Edwardian, the round-edged ones. What size are you?"

"Fourteen."

"Oh, you are small, aren't you! I'm fifteen and a half. Anyway, I've got these Edwardian ones, they're a full three and a half inches. Picked 'em up down Portobello Market. Well...the collars were yellow. I got them starched twice and they come up beautiful shining white and so stiff, absolutely marvellous. Cut the neck off me. I adore them."

He laughed, tossing back that shiny head, catching a glimpse of himself in a mirror. (A round, gilt-edged mirror.)

"Now listen, I've got an antique starched shirt I can't get into anymore but you certainly could. It's a fourteen and a half. Know the type? You've got to pull it over your head."

"Uh huh."

"Perhaps you'd like it. Well, I'd love to meet you. Maybe a Tuesday. I go to the gym Monday, Wednesday and Friday. Or perhaps a Thursday? Yeah. No. Let's say Tuesday. Six okay? And what do you look like? Oh, and where?"

"The shop?"

"Um, how about..."

"How about the Barbican Centre, by the fountains?"

"I know the spot you mean. Opposite City of London School for Girls. I think there's a statue there, isn't there? A running man or a black horse or something."

"Something like that."

Nothing like that in fact and far too symbolic to mention to the man. Hamish landed on my shoulder and said, "Piss off!" in Jessie's tone of voice unusually loudly. This went unheard as Graeme said:

"Okay. Six, on the dot. So, John, what do you look like?"

"Do you want the full turn-on description or just the edited highlights?"

He chortled, perhaps wanting the turn-on edited highlights.

"I'm tall, just over six foot. Short, dark, well-groomed hair. I stick a bit of oil on it."

"Oh, I love greased hair. Don't like that gel stuff on a man, can't run your fingers through it. Go on."

"Clean shaven. Slim, always have been. Public School education. An all boys establishment in West London."

There was a long slow mmm-ing sound over the phone. An escort agency would have given full marks for attitude.

"Thought so, you speak so nicely. Did you have stiff collars there?"

I paused, letting him imagine the white lines of a sports

pitch, ropes swinging in the gym, a locker room, sound of the showers. Woody smell, boy smell. Benediction on bended knees, incense. Italic nibs, swoosh of the cane.

"Not when I attended, Graeme."

"I've had this fetish since I was sixteen, you know. I used to think I was the only one. Then I did the ad and there are others. Loads. I even wrote to Millivres asking them to do a pin-up peel off, dressed formally, in one of their magazines. Got a very sniffy letter back. It took years before I told my friends, you know, cos my friends are much younger than me. And when I told them they said okay. Fine. You know, like it wasn't such a big deal. I was quite closetty about it, see? I felt a bit embarrassed."

I didn't answer this, absorbed with Hamish who'd returned to my shoulder, straining forward in the hope I'd allow him to stick his little head inside my mouth to delicately drink warm saliva.

"Have you ever answered an ad before?"

"Never ever. Cross my heart and hope to die."

"Ever placed one?"

"No, but it's worth considering."

Hamish winked at me, then flew off, landing on the Yamaha to look out at sky.

Some dog had a good bark for the duration of our brief rendezvous the following Tuesday. The dog belonged to a Swiss girl called Elizabeth who I'd got chatting to when I arrived. She was a little distressed, crying on the bench farthest from the crowds, by the last fountain which had weak water pressure and spluttered. I asked if I could help. She asked for a cigarette. I bought her a pack. I didn't dare tell her everything would be alright.

She was ignored when Graeme arrived, five minutes late, wearing jeans, a Polo open neck, carrying a soft grey leather jacket under his arm. He dragged along a certain mood with him, like he'd just received results of a blood sample taken two weeks back. There was quite a shine on his brogues and bald head. No smile. Perhaps he'd seen me talking to the girl, had spotted the bubble around us. Maybe he'd even caught a glimpse of her reddened eyes and was suspicious. We both stared across green water at a church covered with plastic sheeting the colour of pale, frosted glass.

We shook hands, but it was the hello-goodbye contact of an executioner. I wore a plain, single-breasted suit. Silver grey. Ox blood brogues. Graeme looked at my blue cotton Oxford button-down shirt collar like it was a passage of air into which he could make a deep deep dive, but wouldn't. It had been Ray's favourite shirt, the one he'd been wearing when we first met.

The unfashionably tight clothing revealed the well-defined body he was fighting to preserve. Maybe he hadn't expected me to turn up. He certainly didn't have much to say, he'd burned himself out on the phone. As a body I think I was quite acceptable, but he didn't go much on my soul.

"Graeme, you mentioned that you'd like a step-by-step striptease spread in a wank magazine. Who'd be your ideal model. Richard Gere? Keanu Reeves?"

He could have punched me on the nose. He gathered up his jacket: "I'd love to dress Bruce Willis formally—top hat and tails, white gloves—and photograph him before a full-length mirror peeling off, going ever so slowly on the studs, braces, laces and buttons."

Even this failed to get smiling eye contact from me, though I was curious about the look on his face as he said, "Then I'd thrash his arse until it bled. I hope you find what you're looking for young man."

He seemed to be clenching his buttocks very tightly as he walked away. I wonder if he watched from a distance to see what I did once he'd evacuated the meeting point. He wouldn't have liked what he saw. Wiping my brow, I returned to the space beside the Swiss girl and one stroke of her cross-breed dog's neck quietened it like he was mine. We looked more like lovers than strangers meeting for the second time in half an hour. She lived in Cricklewood and was an estimated nine weeks pregnant. If she had she told me that earlier I wouldn't have bought her the cigarettes.

Before he burst into my ear there was some late-night, long-distance static which came to be a tell-tale sign of his calls. These calls also ended with that long-distance pip, probably something he wasn't aware of. The pip can be soothing and sweet sometimes, a cute fullstop to a conversation. Not with this caller though. Through the crackle and grit, more suited to Tierra del Fuego than Cambridgeshire, he had access. Dai was his name (pronounced die, as in Die bitch!) but he preferred to be called David.

He'd been careful, years back, to swap that Welsh accent of his for a nondescript educational drone. Only when excited or angry did it thicken his voice. Just one look at the man's handwriting would have steered me clear of that closet case.

"Is that Owen?"

Though my eyes scanned the sheet above the phone, I guessed it was the Welsh Chap who'd advertised in *The Pink Paper*. I smiled very wide. "Yes."

"Ah, my name's David. I'm calling from March in Cambridgeshire. I had a card off you yesterday in reply to my ad in *The Pink*. Does this mean anything to you?"

"Oh, yes. Hi. Thanks for phoning."

"How are you?"

For some daft reason I turned a blind eye to the edginess lurking beneath his well-practiced cheery voice, his shortness of breath, the close proximity of his teeth to the mouthpiece.

"Right then lad, what can I say to you? I'll be coming down to London every Wednesday for a year as from July. Starts in July, the course does. Um, I just wanted to meet people from London, really. I'll finish round four, see. As my expenses are paid I thought I could see a bit of London. Now then, what I've got is...I've a week's holiday next week and I'm coming to London one day but I can't stay too late as I'll have to get the eight thirty to get the Peterborough connection at nine fifty. When can we meet?" he asked.

"Perhaps next week some time, for tea."

"Where? Wednesday alright with you? I'll be up Gower Street way filling out forms and gettin' things sorted. Finding out where everything is, taking a look about like.

Maybe we could meet at Kings Cross station. Wednesday?"

"Wednesday's fine, but Kings Cross is not the best place to get a cuppa. How about the base of Nelson's column?"

"How will I recognise you?"

"I'll be all in white on a mountain bike. I'm 22, tall, with slicked-back dark hair."

"Rather a dramatic meeting place," he said, excited and imagining. "But...oh no," he continued, "...that'll do. Right then. What time on Wednesday?"

"Four thirty. By the lions, right at the base."

"You will turn up? You are genuine?"

"You can trust me."

"I'll be wearing..."

"Don't say. If you don't like the look of me and want to forget it, you can. I'll wait up to half an hour, then be off."

"That's...I know what you mean...that's kind but...We could go for a meal, my treat."

"Let's just call it tea for the moment, eh? What's your line? I guess it has to be Medicine or Education if you're going to be over in Gower Street."

"Education. I'm a school inspector for Humanities and the National Curriculum is doing my head in!"

It was more than the National Curriculum that was doing the man's head in. We met as arranged. He wore a raincoat on what turned out to be a sweltering day. If there is such a thing as a God and if s/he gives merit marks, then there should be half a dozen gold stars on my page for befriending the Welsh lonely heart of D fucking Parry. What my mum would call a really nice man. His neighbours would probably agree. A nicely clipped lawn, washing out on a Monday, lights out by eleven. A man who keeps himself to himself. The sort of description given by neighbours framed in their hallways speaking to news crews after the discovery of the latest serial killer or schoolroom mass murderer.

There's a refreshment hut in St James' Park, opposite the ICA. We had tea there. His eyes studied the male torso printed on my white teeshirt promoting The Smiths' first release. The rolled-up sock down the front of my white Levi's also gained eye-popping attention.

His blushing was close to haemorrhage, his breathing a concern, his skin a heavy challenge to deodorant spray. All this was made less repulsive by the taste and soft fleshy texture of sweet sultanas in my Danish.

I gave him my name, not sure why. My real name, my full name. Being ex-directory, it felt safe. I didn't give him my address, but careful questioning let me slip out mention of Camden Passage, just up the road next to Angel tube. There aren't a lot of Hanmores in Ealing, either. I let too many details slip. When he asked about my parents I told a lot of horrible truths.

He'd had the usual quota of heartbreaks which he sketched at low volume as I walked him around the Photographers' Gallery. He seemed harmless, easy enough to swat away. I waved him goodbye at Leicester Square tube and forgot about him as I browsed in Dillons. He'd been in search of someone to love (or hate) for a long time.

Interflora guarantees satisfaction with their vast selection of beautifully arranged flowers, same-day delivery if the order's placed before one pm. At four the delivery man looked embarrassed as he handed over a large, cellophane-wrapped apricot card with a floral display of creams, yellows and pinks bursting through its oval front window. *Living Card.*

It felt like a fuse wire had been lit and the hissing had begun. It had been three days since I'd met Dai. The card read:

D
(Dai/David)
Remember me?
Letter to follow.

The letter came the following day.

–, –––– Rd,
March,
Cambridgeshire
Tel: 01354 –––

Liam,

Surprise! Surprise!
Just a short note to let you know what I felt following our first meeting. The very fundamental thing is to say YES, I did enjoy it very much. I couldn't go through it all again so when I got home I destroyed the other seven replies to my ad. My name is Dai as you know, but please call me David. I'd be delighted to hear from you very soon and look forward to it. For two people to meet for the first time ever is quite an ordeal, I suppose, but I must say that as soon as I saw you I felt some warmth. Believe you me, if you had been otherwise you would probably still be cycling round Nelson's Column. You handled the tour very well. I'd never been to that photographic gallery.
Tomorrow I am going to Wales for the weekend to stay with my sister. Anyway, I have waffled on enough and all I really wanted to say was thanks for your kindness and I hope that we can do it again. It was kind of you to treat me to tea. My treat next time. Dinner, on me. (If you want a next time, that is.) Hope you like the flowers.
Look after yourself now lad.
(I do hope you'll phone.)
All the very best.
Yours,
D

PS You're probably wondering how I got your address. I've got a friend who works for British Telecom and he gave it me. Hope you don't mind.

I remembered the shiny black of his eyes. Dogs get that look when they want to screw or when they see something they're desperate to consume. An extremely rapid succession of unwanted communications had begun.

Hamish tip-toed up to the top of my head and, once in a while, banged his beak against a headphone ear-piece, curious about the sound leaking out.

I didn't like the AUTO HARMONY, a feature which automatically added cloying harmony notes to a melody played. I never selected any of the five different types of harmony.

The Creative American Female replied on darkest purple paper in silver ink. Maybe that's the way they do things in Pittsburgh.

PO BOX —
Pittsburgh
USA

Dear Uri,
Thanks for your letter!
London is my destination, although a few months away, 4-6 in fact. Unfortunately I've had to delay a trip there until my financial future warrants moving to a foreign country.
Being that you photograph and write about your culture, I'm sure you can be of assistance to me. I want to video your city in my free time. I'd like to know where the best shots may be taken from an artistic point of view. Could you assist me there do you think?
I've decided to go to London because I feel it offers a culture where social concern is still abundant unlike Pittsburgh where everyone appears apathetic.
If you'd care to comment on your social culture be it zestful or dull—please do. I'll give you my view of the city where I live as a waitress at the moment. Write soon if possible as my curiosity is unruly.
Take care!
Kathy

Verdict: I considered an aerogram on UK decay but didn't write back, then lived in fear of a knock at the door from a waitress wielding a video camera, suffering a financial crisis and seeking assistance.

Now, Janis was a girl. She gave me all the inside stories of life in the record department of a South London branch of Woolworths. One particular perk is discount on the discounts. She adores clearance sales. She replied with speed, blunt pencil on pink.

—, ——— Close,
Abbey Wood

Dear Patrick,

Thanks for the line + the offer to phone you after I advertised in Time Out. Can't phone you yet, my phone won't be on until next month. Will this letter do? Hope so.
Well, this should reach you by Wednesday with luck so how about calling round my flat Friday eve? About 7, after I've finished my hard days work. I'll play you some of my favourite records.
See you Friday then.
Don't let this sensitive woman down!!

Janis.

Verdict: Crazy. But the tv pages didn't fill me with excitement, so I decided to turn up on her doorstep as suggested.

I wore the same silver-grey suit I'd worn for the baldy not so far back, same shirt. I still cycled. Having worn cycle shorts and teeshirts for weeks, a suit felt awkward and heavy.

There wasn't a spyhole in the front door, a council flat irregularity. No darkening of the small dot of glass to give a once-over. Instead, the letter-box opened like a cat-flap.

"Hello," the voice whispered. "Who is it?"

Any melody in her voice had been scraped away with nicotine. She sounded like a cartoon mad woman. The fake name had slipped from my mind, I nearly said Bike Boy.

"It's me," I whispered.

I bent to eye level, gave her a winning three-stage smile.

"Didn't think you'd come," she said more to herself as she eyed me carefully.

"Hello."

Once vetted, okayed, I was in.

She was older than the advertised age of twenty nine. She'd lopped off a lot of unhappy years. She had the look of an obstinate middle-aged man got up in bad drag. A dim, fly-specked lightbulb treated my senses to brown Paisley wallpaper and canary yellow glossed doors.

"Didn't think you'd come. Place is a mess. I'd've tidied up a bit." She gave up-from-the-cauldron laughter, as if she realised that a bit would not have been enough.

I sat on a filthy three-seater sofa. Plastic. To my left a pile of Casualty Department women's magazines. To my right a pile of intimately stained knickers and beige bras. Three record players dominated the room: a polished new one with a CD; a tired-out Sony of mediocre-to-poor quality and an old Dansette, a possible collector's item ruined with the same canary yellow gloss. She made a cup of tea in a corner while I endured Iron Maiden at considerable volume from the mediocre player.

Her long bleached hair, worn in an untidy bun, would have suited her better down. Despite the squalor she seemed quite a happy sad soul. She spent a lot of loose change on discount jewellery.

"I love photography. It's my number one hobby. Look at these."

She'd started. I witnessed the last three years' unhappy collaboration between her, an old Zenith and Woolies' photographic department. Prints galore of East End scenes, architectural decay being her big delight. She's in the right country for that. Many of the photos had sticky smudges on them like they'd been passed round at a kiddies' party.

"You *are* gay, I hope. You don't look very gay. Not, you know..."

"Queeny."

"Yes."

"I do my best."

"You've got a nice face, Patrick. I'll take your picture."

Pulling all three sets of roller blinds down, she eyed me with cruel speculation: *Can I get him to put some make-up on?* Rhythms the universe is not used to hearing began to pound in that room which had the not unfamiliar stink of my mother's handbag in the early seventies. She wanted a picture to show her mates at work.

This photograph was taken half an hour later after I'd talked ASA speeds and how to adjust the camera for different film types and conditions. Tips on focusing in low light, the use of *f* stops. She nodded and said, "I see…" when she didn't really, then asked me to smile. I gave the desired pose and expression: cute, with a heavy hint of faggot. The camera waited at the foot of her chair, *ON* flashing.

We looked at the response to her ad. A chap named Chris, aka Christine, had written seeking tips on hair and make-up. Poor Christine, in need of a good hot meal, fresh air and at least eight hours a night, alone, in clean white sheets for a month. State.

"This one's in Venice. Look! Very butch. Don't like the look of him. And this one, well, just plain boring."

Someone, had to be male, started having a very audible piss. I was just that little bit alarmed, the way you get when a restaurant bill is so much more than you'd estimated. My hostess turned to me:

"My brother. It's okay. He keeps himself to himself. He only comes in here to listen to music. That's his machine there, the new one. He keeps his headphones in his room, in a box, the box they come in. Hardly ever goes out 'cept to sign on. If he wants something he gets it out of the Argos. Spends his time drawing cartoons on his computer, mostly. Twenty eight. But he's good company and makes a wicked omelette when he's in the mood. Can we do another picture? Your fringe has flopped down a bit and looks pretty."

Flash. Shot against the wall.

"Shall I take one of you, Janis?"

"But I've got no make-up on!" She rolled her eyes like a ventriloquist's dummy at the very idea. I was intrigued with the bloodshot whites of her eyes, yellowed like a sheep's.

She put on her little bit of fake, lots of it. Street-market bargains at prices difficult to resist. Colours improbable on a woman outside of Turkey. Lipstick the colour Jessie next door paints her front step. How she ever expected the baked-bean foundation to lay happily on so much Nivea I do not know. On went a brazen shawl, fairground prize earrings and a pair of tarty slingbacks. While she had her back turned I pocketed a Gary Glitter CD and a pair of dirty pink knickers, then breathed heavily on the camera lens.

Focusing on her exceptionally thin lips I saw her look change from shifty to ever so slightly sensuous, then quickly back again.

"I feel safe with my brother here. He won't let me open the door unless he's here."

I had the feeling the brother was listening behind the frosted glass door. The lights had gone off in the hall so I couldn't judge the shadows, but she probably knew his ways. To the total stranger, the man with CD and stinky pink knickers in his pocket, knife inside his pannier, she said:

"You can't be too careful nowadays, you know."

I sipped the fortifying Diet Coke only after she'd had half a glass first. She also served cracked biscuits and stale jam tarts. All around the room there was food, junk food. A sachet of blancmange powder lay beside the knickers. Dolly mixtures dribbled out of a bag on to the window-sill. Pink wafers on the tv looked dry and dusty.

"Be a love and put a record on."

Three shelves spilled blasts from the past: Culture Club, Cockney Rebel, Patsy Cline, Status Quo, Abba, Christmas novelties and a signed Cilla Black. The majority were marked SALE, REDUCED or CLEARANCE.

"The council came seven years ago to mend the kitchen sink and my copy of *Paper Roses* by Marie Osmond went missing. I'd played it that very morning. I only noticed a month later. Had to be them. No one else had been in. I felt very sad. I bought that record my first week at Woolworths. I didn't tell my brother, he would've killed 'em."

I may have been blushing or blanching fast so I looked

above the dirty fireplace which sported examples of coiled pottery, brassy doo-dahs, plain brown envelopes behind a clock and a row of half eaten chocolate bars. In large print were two messages:

New wallpaper needed
Nothing will make me forget you.

"Forget who?" I asked. It was a simple question which instantly unlocked stored-away tales.

"I worked in a dry cleaners. We were always getting part-timers from the agency down when there was a rush on. This Romford boy, Si, was so sweet. We got on really well. Gay. Got on brilliant. The rest ribbed him. It really left a gap in my life when the holidays were up and he went back to university to study French. I feel an affinity with gays."

She paused, looking around my eyes, not deep into them. This made a change.

"Do..."

"Yes?"

"Do you wear make-up? You've got a pretty face. Do you?"

"No."

"You should. You'd look lovely with a bit on. Do you dress up?"

"Only in black skin-tight cycle shorts."

"What?"

"Just kidding."

"Oh."

"I did a few times when I was nine or ten."

"I was just wondering." (Persuasively.) "It'd suit you."

I think she was coaxing me to try on her little bits of glam. I sat with my legs a little wider apart, and breathed in with a loud sniff.

"One of the guys who replied wrote that he had fresh breath. Now, what kind of thing is that for a gay guy to come out with to a *sensitive woman*? Could you...would you do me a favour?" She leaned forward, whispered for emphasis: "Would you take me to a gay club, please? Heaven. I want to go to Heaven. I hear it's the largest gay disco in Europe. Oh, please. I've got a few days off next week. We could meet outside. I know where it is. I went there once but chickened out in the queue. I'd have to leave by one or I'd be dead for a week. What do you say?"

"Blimey. Okay. Saturday's best. Busiest. Meet you outside at eleven, this Saturday?"

"Lovely. You're a pal. Eleven, this Saturday."

The arrangement was duly entered into her little Snoopy diary, the first entry for weeks.

"I get lazy about things. When I get my phone I can call the guys who answer my ads. No privacy out there, though. I prefer to write and get 'em round. I need a spyhole. Brother doesn't want to know. He's got a drill, but he just keeps it in his room, in the box it come in. Put another record on."

Deciding to play something truly hideous, I was faced with over-choice. I settled on a Bon Jovi single. When I turned she was taking a bite out of a Snickers from the fire-place. She had a strange stomach, making her look four months pregnant. Some sort of bowel inflammation, perhaps. As the record started, she got this far off look in her eyes and pounded the arm-rest of her chair: "Ooh! I love this. Saw 'em at Hammersmith Odeon with a gay rocker I know. Great!"

It was time to go.

"I'm glad you're leaving early, actually. I like to be in bed by ten."

I kissed her lightly on the cheek and coughed very loudly before opening the door, giving the brother ample warning.

"Bye ducks," she said, waving ta-ta.

Mad cow. Around the corner I took off the suit, folding it neatly into a carrier bag before packing it into the pannier. It would have to be cleaned. The shirt came off, too—destined for a boil-wash. Sitting on the kerb, swapping brogues for the Sidi Dominators, I saw a face up at a window. It didn't take much to work out that it was her brother. If a policeman asked me to describe the face I'd have to say I couldn't. It was too dark, officer.

My nipples hardened in the breeze. Towards Plumstead Common my legs decided to ease up on catching sight of a jogger. The occasional intensity of headlights made the easy, regular motions of the limbs more filmic. I was instantly hard. He couldn't hear the gentle click of chain, pedals or gears. I cycled alongside awhile, letting him give my recently shaved body the once over before making eye contact.

"Nice night for it," he said.

I smiled at this, the oldest of lines. Speeding ahead I didn't look back. When I came to an area where the bushes thickened, just beyond his line of vision, I turned off my lights. Resting the bike down into long grass, my breathing began to quicken. Stroking my penis lightly through the pink knickers, waiting for him, I felt terribly excited.

'Thanks. Lovely evening. See you Saturday, 11pm.'

I signed the card with my awful full name, Liam Patrick Hanmore. Writing '(Patrick to my friends)' beneath was a detail, a precaution in case I bumped into anyone I knew. Fake names can be such a nuisance.

She didn't turn up. No note. No phone call. Nothing. Maybe she'd spotted the missing CD or knickers. There could be a lot of maybes.

March, Cambridgeshire.

The recurrent postmark announced the arrival of cards made from the wood pulp of managed Scandinavian forests. The cards were always sent first class, catching a six thirty post, always Price Code F, never a pleasure to receive.

I'm glad you're my friend the italics on the outside whined.

*Chances are...*the italics on the inside whispered...*that when you open this card—I'll be thinking of you.*

Each card was initialled with an angular *D* in black ink.

Having spent a month of smoke-filled evenings designing the ad, each innuendo atop his tongue for hours, failed phrases binned in temper, he'd finally reached the strokes of words which cast a spell—for him. He expected one hell of a lot in exchange for that cheque he'd sent off to *The Pink Paper*. What he was getting was the most painful foreplay. He very much liked what he'd met. He thought I was bona, drop dead G. A time-bomb of madness was ticking away in his head. He wanted dick.

Lying in the dark with nothing but my headphones on, I didn't hear the phone ringing until a pause between tracks. I'd forgotten to put the answerphone on.

"I want to speak to Sidney."

"Yes, speaking," two words delivered with artificial reticence.

"This is Sidney speaking?"

"Yes."

The voice was firm, hard, matter of fact.

The School Master was scary, his polite, clipped English very much to the point. It took a while before I could get a word in edgeways.

"Ah. Right. Well...first I inspect a pupil to make sure he's up to standard. Then I ask that pupil, having passed the preliminary tests, to strip down for further inspection in my study. This way I can ascertain exactly what that pupil requires. I'd have to put you over my knee and spank you first. Then you'd dress up in a schoolboy uniform, which is absolutely compulsory. Then you'd suck my dick—see what goes on from there. Understand my meaning? Your typical Head. I have lots of straight boys round. Quite normal. I'm not gay myself. Once a boy comes round they usually come again. Come back for more as they know what they're gonna get. I hope you'll come over soon, very soon. I'll pay for a cab if you like. Come over for a good thrashing like a good naughty boy." (Pause.) "Come on over for the thrashing of your life, you little slut an' slave. I'll make you work real hard. It'll be Sir and Beg!" (Pause.) "But for now I want you to tell me a bed-time story. It's called Do You Remember? Okay?...You're eight, nine, eleven, thirteen...you choose how old, nothing beyond fifteen though—"

Fuck this for a game of marbles, I thought. Hoping what I was about to say would ring reasonably true, I took a deep breath which probably got him all excited.

"Um, this is a bit awkward. Yes, my name is Sidney, well, Sid. But I didn't reply to your ad, or any ad. Some joker replied to a whole batch of ads giving my name and number. My phone's been going all hours of the day and night. I'm going to have to get British Telecom to intercept cos it's

CALL ME

getting a bit much. I'm sorry you've been inconvenienced the same way I've been for the last two weeks."

I thought I'd done pretty well. My drama teacher would have been proud.

"Are you having me on? Are you sure you aren't just chickening out? Are you? You sound very nice. Are you for rent? Is that it? Prostitute poofter?"

"This is all a mistake."

"Wank a lot do you, Sidney? I can tell you're queer."

"I'm going to put the phone down now."

"Listen, you've got me all turned on. I'm playing with myself. I've got my big dick out. If you did reply and you're just turning chicken, you time wasting little shit, I hope you...I'd...I'd like to kick your pretty little head in. Hear me? Kick Sid's pretty little head in!"

He slammed the phone down.

"Oh, go fill some teeth or whatever you do," I said in a tired voice.

The phone rang immediately, making me jump. Someone blew a raspberry. Then the phone rang again. It was Jessie. Her brother had died unexpectedly. I was delighted. She was going to have to stay up for the funeral. Hamish was to stay a while longer.

"Kieran?"

"Speaking."

"Oh, I got a note from you today because of an ad."

"Oh, thanks for phoning."

"It took me completely by surprise."

As did the Satin Man's accent.

"Placed the ad ages ago, see? You just caught the three month deadline."

"So, you're the thirty two year old, slim, attractive, muscular guy into satin. From Ireland by the sounds of it."

"What a good memory you have! Yes, from Kerry originally, but now I live Greenford. West West London."

Next to Ealing, queen of the suburbs, where I grew up.

"I'm not long, all that long...well, it's nearly twelve months now, a year ago now...a year since I split up from a relationship going on for seven years. Monogamous. I'm in a phone-box at the moment because I share with another guy and I'd... he's straight. I feel a bit awkward talking with him about, see?"

"I get the picture. I was intrigued by your ad."

"Oh, yeah. My interest. Well," (big smile entering his voice), "I love it. I've had a very poor response, actually. No one genuinely interested in satin or nylon. So, have you got any satin gear yourself?"

"I used to be a competitive cyclist but, well, you know. It was one injury after another. Anyway, yes. I've got some lovely shiny rayon an' stuff. Shorts an' the like."

"Oh, that sounds really good. Those cycle shorts, they fascinate me. They're so...especially when I'm driving past them and the cyclists are raised above the saddle. It's the sheen—really, um, really..."

"I've got one top, kind of silver grey it is, which is really shiny. It's got a kind of metallic sheen to it."

"Sounds great. I'm Finbar by the way. I'll give you a description: I'm about five foot eleven. Tall. I've got loads of gear. Loads. Costs me a fortune! I must have forty pairs of football shorts. I'm also into jockey riding gear but way too big to wear it meself. And windsurfing gear, that's a new direction for me. I loved the winter Olympics this year, if you know what I mean. And, er...what about you?"

"I'm quite a normal lad really."

(Very interested.) "Yeah?" (Always works.)

"Recently twenty two, tall, slim. Not a hair on my body, except a bush of silky pubes I'd like you to stick your nose up against."

(Pause).

"What colour's your hair?"

"Dark. Goes jet black with oil on. I like oil."

"Very nice. The sheen on a guy's body turns me on too."

"What's your line, Finbar?"

"Manager of a bakery in Hayes. Want to have my own place again one day. I used to, see, with my lover. When we split up we sold up. So, shall we meet up? I'm not a promiscuous person."

"How about a swim at Northolt baths? My favourite pool. That's close to you. Sunday morning in Speedos?"

(Pathetically.) "I can't swim. I could meet you there if you like."

"Something else perhaps."

"I did learn one time but I'm just one of those people who just doesn't take to water. I can do the doggy paddle."

"I'm sure you can. We could always check into a cheap hotel for an evening."

"No, I don't really like that idea."

I pursued this line of discomfort. It was time to discard, shoot to kill: "Oh, I've done that loads of times before. It saves on the laundry if you want some dirty fun, you know."

"Dirty fun?"

"Yeah, you know. A bit of shit an' piss. I love the look of a drop of yellow cascading down a guy's face."

There was a long pause before he put the phone down, ever so gently.

Jessie's got a friend, Mrs Hitchin. A nosy old cow with an aversion to flying creatures. She was happy enough to water Jessie's plants every other day but would sooner eat Hamish roasted than look after him for a day or two. Before I went out on to the landing, I could see the bitch watering the stringy geraniums outside Jessie's front door with a teapot.

"'Old on a minute, Liam. Something came for you earlier. Didn't you hear your bell go?"

Yes, you nosey old cow. I did hear the fucking bell go and I chose to ignore it. But I didn't say that. I'm a nice chap. Nice decent and respectable, keeping myself to myself, keeping the communal staircase and piss swilling lift nice. Lights out by eleven.

"I was on the balcony, cleaning the windows. Didn't hear a thing."

"I'll just get your little surprise."

"Oh, thanks. That's very kind of you, Mrs H."

She returned with the box I'd seen her take with such interest just ten minutes back, through the spyhole. She was beaming.

"How nice it is to have an admirer!" She winked as she shut Jessie's door, going back inside to poke through drawers and use the phone. I didn't like her or her parting line. She knew about Ray and me.

It was an attractive little box, containing a single red rose in one section, a scroll in another. I opened it next to the rubbish shute.

It's so nice to know you're there.

D

Not liking what he was saying with flowers, I disposed of the unique same day delivery. Down it went, garbage. That's what his single red rose had become, without entering my little home. But even down in the massive, grey garbage cans, I was troubled by that rose. Even after the disposal men came on Tuesday, all scrunched up and dumped on a heap, those petals still managed to exist. Reduced to something small, compressed and rotten—with all the other bits and pieces trashed—they were still fuming up into the air, polluting it, visiting trouble. I should have phoned him.

"Luke?"

"Speaking."

"Got your reply to my ad." He sounded like he probably had lots of initials after his name.

"I answered a few. Which one are you then?"

This put him on the spot and made me sound like an above average slag.

"It was in *Capital Gay*. A leather ad. Looking for a younger guy into leather."

His lips must have been on the mouthpiece. His voice went straight into my head, like he was breathing all over me. It was neither seductive nor terrifying.

"Right," I said, "go on."

"And how old are you Luke?"

"Old enough to know better."

"And exactly how old is that?"

"Twenty three."

"And what sort of things do you enjoy?"

"You tell me."

"Well, I enjoy...I obviously enjoy dominating younger guys who, um, enjoy being submissive and, er, dominated. Getting them to do boot-licking and, er, putting a dog collar on them and taking them for a walk over Hampstead Heath or out in the country. In a secluded spot I could push you down and humiliate you—take your clothes off, make you crawl through mud, force you to see to my boots, suck cock, lick arse. Um...and generally make you pine and work for things. Whatever you wanted you'd have to work for. I'm in Muswell Hill. You are, I take it, in Clerkenwell."

"You've checked the code. How thorough."

He couldn't act tough the way he would have liked, but he was trying.

"I work in the City. I pass through Clerkenwell every day."

I greeted this with silence. Clerkenwell: a place of doctor's coats and butchers' aprons and City boys in suits with ties. Sodomite territory.

"Do you know the leather shop, Expectations?"

"Yeah."

"I buy there, there and The Zipper Store in Camden. Buy toys for boys like you. I've got a harness you'd look good in, feel great in. You name it. My most expensive purchase lately was a pair of riding boots. I'd like your tongue to break them in." (Pause.) "I'm not too rough. Wouldn't break your ribs or anything like that, unless you wanted me to. Mild stuff really. Fantasy, but...let's see what develops. Could you...could you come round tonight?"

"I won't be peed on."

"That's a pity, but okay."

The night was sultry, the hour dangerous.

"What's the address?"

I was there, in the north London suburb of Muswell Hill, middle class and residential, forty minutes later. A place of placid thoughtless routines and the occasional juicy bit of gossip.

In the elevator to the third floor as instructed, I realised I didn't even know his name. It was after midnight. He stood, by the door, silent, smoking a cigarette. Sandy hair, six foot, hadn't caught the sun in a while. Regular features but for an extremely full mouth and a recent vertical scar by his right eye. Slightly stooped, a little pock-marked. Black leather shining. Your average scene queen begging for it.

I walked straight on in without wiping my feet, inflicting mild abuse on the cream carpet. Pulling the REM teeshirt up, over the shoulders then off my body, hot and very slightly panting from the ride, I fell back into one of the two large institution armchairs which faced each other in the middle of the room. This seemed to surprise him. The lacey antimacassars certainly were a surprise to me.

It was smoggy as Venus in there. He'd obviously been smoking all evening. When he shut the door behind me he smiled like Death's welcome. Behind the smile uneven teeth, browned at the edges, spoilt the allure of the too-generous mouth, full lips waiting for a kiss.

On a shelf over an electric fire, previous generations of the man's family smiled into the darkness of the room. The fire effect provided a slow rotating orange glow through the room, but the bars were off. The radiators were on high, even though the night was warm to humid. In cosy little homes like this, late night callers lose their minds, antibody status and ability to breathe.

I put my feet up on a narrow black table between a tall, thick candle veined with past spillage and a black leather jock strap. A tv flickered the pale flesh tones of a blond youth getting an efficient fisting from a masked muscle man.

Silent by the screen, more slave than master, he licked his lips, perhaps envying the fist. Silent. The muscle man withdrew his forearm for viewers all over the world to witness the challenging length and thickness of the rubber-gloved limb. The hand was reinserted with seeming ease to root about inside the living body.

The blond youth took a sniff of poppers as the forearm vanished. The look on his face suggested that giving good ass is not as easy as it looks. His writhing, twisting and soft murmur of complaints confirmed this. (There's nothing funny about a prolapsed rectum.) The camera didn't linger, cutting swiftly to the unexpressive, oozing rear orifice.

Semi-erect, I dropped my shorts, putting on the leather

jock I guessed he wanted me in. Opening all three sets of venetian blinds, he eyed me with speculation: *What the fuck's he up to?* The candle flame doubled size with the slow entry of fresh air. The copulating rhythm of the universe began to pound in that room which had an unfamiliar smell, perhaps spilled poppers which joss sticks struggled to disperse. I turned to him and smiled.

"Fancy a drink?" he asked.

A monotone voice. Maybe behind these bland icy words was the idea of a cocktail of Irish Cream coffee and seven crushed sleeping pills. Maybe not.

"No. No thanks."

Something moved in a corner—a Corgi, watching out of one eye, hoping there'd be no shouting, no slapping around. Perhaps this dog was the only warm influence in the man's life. Perhaps not. He put on a shiny new CD of an old hit, Tubular Bells.

"Don't ask me any questions because there's nothing interesting for me to say about myself. Let's just do it."

He made quite a business of pulling on a peaked leather cap and large, thick motor-cycle gloves, more like boxing gloves with that heavy-duty protective ribbing over the knuckles. It was as if he were going somewhere, off on a journey somewhere special and secret.

Removing a chair from the dining table, I spotted a gas bill in the name of a JG Cuerden who owed sixty seven pounds ninety six for the last quarter. I put the chair against one of the more heavily greased walls. He said nothing. Like a minion, I hunched before the chair. He stepped on my back on his short trip up to the seat. He didn't know what the hell he'd let into the flat but seemed to like what was happening. Still he said nothing.

The knife reflected candlelight upon my face as I removed the polish and brush from my pannier. The boots were brand new, they didn't need much of a rub, but for a full ten minutes that's what I did. Rubbed away.

"They say the best way is with spit and polish, boy."

"Yes, Sir."

"Yeah, use that tongue, boy."

He'd obviously been getting quite a diet of porn. So there I was on my hands and knees, spreading well-educated saliva over his expensive recent purchase. He started making those porno sounds, faking it at first, then getting carried away with the role play, thrusting his hips forward as he leaned against the wall.

"How's that, Sir?"

"Not good enough."

He'd had time to think. Perhaps we'd reached a part in Tubular Bells where he felt comfortable or inspired. At home.

"Against the wall. Now!"

Declining the offer of handcuffs behind my back, I played along with his doggy fantasy by consenting to wear a large dog collar. The chinkle-chankle of the chain didn't get his dog at all excited, as I'd expected. The dog knew she wasn't the one off for walkies.

"Crawl, you mutt!"

Pulling of the leash made the collar uncomfortably tight as he became more excited. I was given a guided tour of the man's one-bedroom flat, mercifully carpeted but poorly hoovered, ending up in the bedroom. Lying face-down on the man's orthopaedic mattress, I received a mild pinking of my bottom with the flat of his right hand. Maybe he just wanted some intimate tactile contact, avoiding the embarrassment of affection seeking.

The strokes had a kind of hard, cold softness. Then his tongue savoured the warmth before his whole face was plunged between my Immac-ed buttocks. Even in the doggy position I nearly slipped off to sleep with the slow deep rimming he gave so expertly. His tongue entered, rotating and delving, warm breath heating me up inside and out. Tongue, stroking the nerves gently at first, then harder, becoming alive. Possessed by an angry erotic passion, jabbing the prostate in a fast in-out rhythm. He soon replaced tongue with leather-clad fingers, widening and stretching until he could look in, blow, taste and sniff. At one point I think he had four fingers in (maybe a torch too). I took it blind and dumb, determined to explore, to expose myself to the allure of S&M.

"I've got some rope," he whispered. "It's very soft rope. Would you like to be tied up a little?"

I nearly said yes.

I shook my head. Rolling me over roughly, disappointed I wouldn't be a pretty little bundle, and straddling me just like in the videos, thrusting his leather crotch to my mouth like those spreads in *Dungeon Master*, he seemed to grow in stature. Suddenly his forehead was the colour of polished steel. It was like he had received a power surge. When his mouth went down on mine I smelled, then tasted—me. To leave his mark he gave me a love bite. Behind that tight, black leather, just beyond the zipper, his penis was straining to be released.

He walked me back into the living room, where I returned to bootlicking while he tried to remember tips he'd gained from *Interchain*. Blurred memories swelled the man's mind with desire, memories of pornography in which shining metallic tools ended the suffering of pretty boys. Violent seemed an inappropriate word for such reverential actions.

His penis, unzipped and glistening like a cop's rubber truncheon, was pink and separate from his leather-clad body. When the trousers lowered it bounced forth like a cage-crazy cat. His eyes were on the screen, but he was far off into himself. The video had finished. The screen was black and white jumping dots, lively as a laboratory-manufactured virus. Or a mystery one.

"Don't stop licking those boots, *shithead*!"

I licked the heels, sucked the toe, then—bastard—he pushed his right foot in hard. I froze momentarily and his weight shifted on the chair as he looked down.

My mouth was on fire, ignited by a small nail on the underside of the sole. My lip was ripped. (It swelled beautifully, looked sexy for days.) I tasted blood. He went quiet. *Tubular Bells* faded out. Blood welled up on my bottom lip. I could feel it gather, a heavy, fluid drop. As I raised my head it rolled in a steady line down my chin, and dropped on to my chest.

Another drop fell on the shining black toe of his boot. A

pebble drop plop. I licked it up then raised my head for him to see the blood spread over my tongue. His look told me *REC* and *PLAY* buttons were pushed and capturing what would be rewound and wanked over later.

"I'm going to shoot," he said automaton-like. Maybe this was his natural voice, the voice his secretary, ex-wife, children, pupils, bank manager and wide range of bleary-eyed escorts were used to hearing. He pulled the face of an ugly cartoon character who'd just tasted something sour, tongue touching nose at the peak of orgasm histrionics, then he spasmed, jolted, froze where he was and burst stringy white gobs of himself. Every drop of that man's semen splashed down on to my unfortunate chest.

His face drained of all animation like the power had been cut off. His pale, grey eyes stared out of the open window into the navy blue night. Breeze brought stale refreshment to the sweat on his face. He blinked.

"Thank you," he said.

I wonder what spectres of fantasy flick through the mind of that man during a wank. From his little stage, pelvis still thrust ridiculously forward, shoulders hunched, he watched me lying flat on my back, my wide armspan revealing hairless armpits.

"What's your dog called?"

"Sherry."

The dog's ears rose in an instant.

"Sherry! Here, Sherry. Come on."

The dog approached slowly, wagging tail, unsure of her reception. The animal took a deep sniff into one ear, then found the midnight feast waiting on my chest. Her tongue, so much warmer than a human's, continued licking long after the mess had gone. Which taste was she preferring, master's cum or visitor's blood?

From two metres away came a thin, menacing stare. Perhaps my piss, shit, spit, spunk and vomit laid out in a neat line of separate soup bowls would have been preferable to a single lick of my arse. If I'd dropped down dead in front of him, would my body have been whisked off to the bath to be washed down then studied for days before the stinking

stinking job of dismembering, facilitated by Wagner, rum, black dustbin bags and airspray?

The mouth, not made for smiling, smiled. The candle flickered with another sudden gust as I raised myself up. The director of the nasty production in my head suggested a faint strobe effect.

"Give me your cap," I whispered.

His hair was matted by sweat. His cap, his warmth, foreign on my head.

"Suits you," he said. "Try the jacket."

As he removed the jacket, I removed the dog collar.

I stood on the chair. He was now below, wearing the collar, focusing on that black leather jock strap of his. My penis had remained resolutely flaccid throughout the slapstick, only hardening when the dog licked me. From two metres away his eyes changed colour and focus. Something from somewhere had been summoned up or, more likely, had invaded him. I was dealing with a whole new person. The eyes were sinister. An experienced force, a ferocious cold cruelty. He gave me a long, serious, social worker look.

"There's something missing from your life. Do you know what it is?" he asked.

"Is it God?" I replied.

This put him off his stride. He looked at me as though I was a hopeless case then blurted:

"Love! Friendship! Companionship! Togetherness!"

He stormed off towards the bedroom. Sherry was hiding under a small chest of drawers, eyes begging me to go. I heard the swish of zips and falling leather, heavy urination and a rapid showering technique. Hundreds of lurid tattoos were getting a quick soaping down. On top of the tv I saw a red biro on a cheque card on the open cheque book.

"Tea?" The stranger asked, speeding into the kitchen in a dressing gown and tartan slippers.

"Thanks."

He popped his head through a dainty serving hatch.

"Get down from there, silly. You might fall and hurt yourself! Put a record on. You choose."

I heard the top of a bottle being quietly removed for a

silent drink he wasn't prepared to share.

After stock-taking his collection I chose a single, Laurie Anderson's *O Superman*, promising myself to be out of there by the time the record ended. He put the tea and biscuits down, switched off the tv, sat like a vicar about to have afternoon tea.

The song seemed to laugh at us with its *ha ha ha* as the tea stewed in chipped Royal Doulton. I added milk after I'd seen him add milk to his. I swallowed after he'd swallowed. You can never be too careful.

"*O Superman. O Judge. O Mom and Dad. Mom and Dad.*"

He watched me, maybe fascinated by my throat, the entrance tunnel for food, liquid and air.

Maybe not.

"*Hi, I'm not home right now, but if you want to leave a message*
Just start start talking at the sound of the tone."

As he focused on me, he seemed to blur. We were both tired. It was late. His words began to slow and slur.

"Do you have to go? It would be so nice if you stayed."

He looked towards his red biro on the cheque card on the open cheque book and saw me see this and winked the recently scarred eye.

"*Hello? This is your mother. Are you there? Are you coming home?*"

A tangle of moods came down. The atmosphere changed so suddenly, a power-cut transition which surged me with fear. The room became grave and quiet. I felt I was underground. I wished the velvety armchair I was sitting in would eject me home safely to bed. Tom toms started pounding slow and low in my head, their message: *Get the fuck out!*

His face held a glazed expression for a minute, then his mouth smiled too much and he winked. I wondered what he'd done over the years with those wide, blunt-fingered hands. Over and over the tom toms pounded, gaining speed and volume which only I was hearing. I think.

I wasn't frightened but my pulse rate was fast. His eyes

told me he'd just entered another mode. Large, brightly coloured, elusive butterflies of love or lust or madness released by alcohol and music were infesting the man's head, heart and bowels. I felt he knew what I was thinking, word for word. The mist of whatever his vision was shivered me.

I imagined the severed head of a lightly tanned barboy in the refrigerator beside the semi-skimmed milk. Two more in black plastic bags in the closet, in shorts and singlets, broken strings of beads around their bruised necks. Maybe he'd just showered with a carcass or two behind the exotic bathroom curtain he'd rushed me past.

He didn't smile back when I opened my eyes. He was avoiding eye contact.

Here was a man who, no doubt, felt at home in the midst of flickering candles, incense and silent, grinning skulls, eating swans for Sunday lunch. Was he thinking that or was I?

Did he want to decapitate, dismember, deflesh, destroy, leave me to decompose in the garbage? Best out of here, quick. Did he think that or did I?

If he'd made a charge for me, like a soldier with his bayonet ready for anything, I might have screamed for God or my mother. (Or Ray.) I was filled with true, naked, yellow fear. As he talked, an aimless monologue which even bored him, he seemed silent. As he waved his arms and pulled a pantomime of faces, he seemed still and staring. (He'd got me there with all the skill of a salesman on commission.) Black eels invaded my digestive system. As he talked I thought I saw his hair growing, grey roots suddenly appearing under the sandy fullness. My eyes were heavy.

The sudden barking of his dog in my face broke the mood.

He pointed vaguely to my waist. "You can keep that," he said. "And here's a little something. Now go."

On the landing in the prickly dark silence, I stood clad in nothing but a black leather jock strap. In one hand a pannier containing a stolen knife, in the other shiny black skin-tight cycle shorts, teeshirt and cheque for £60. Payee left blank.

I pressed the down button. The lift, it could have been

fifty stories down, groaned and heaved.

I pressed the button again. I started to count. I held the pannier against my chest and the organs that were thumping towards my throat, the scream that was jamming against the back of my teeth.

In my flat with the door locked behind me, just after sunrise, it was 5:13 am, the day of my birthday. I sang Happy Birthday to a man who was earning himself a pretty impressive CV. A man who was realising he didn't know how lost he was.

Through the spyhole I saw the same delivery man again.

"I'll be out in a moment," I shouted through the door. "Leave it on the mat, would you? Thanks."

When he'd gone I opened the door, still in my pyjamas.

On the doorstep in a shallow wicker basket wrapped in cellophane with an orange ribbon tied high beside a little envelope, in front of a floral display of creams yellows and pinks, sat a pink and white teddy bear: 'Cuddles'. What he'd missed out on for years.

The phone rang.

I picked up the basket with one hand and grabbed the phone with the other, for once hoping it was just my mother wanting to wish me happy birthday and check I was still coming over.

"Hello. Is that Euan?"

"Speaking."

"Oh hi! I'm *Capital Gay* ad 89.20. Michael."

"Mr Strut It!"

"Well, I'm hoping you're Mr Strut It, actually. I'm glad it caught your eye. I'm in Camberwell."

"Bet you've been busy auditioning with your ad."

"So so, only fifteen replies. I had a soldier round in all his uniform, that was nice. I put it in for six weeks. It's so cheap in *Capital Gay*. Now, do you like videos? Blue, you know. I've got six tapes. That'll keep you going! You could have an eighteen-hour marathon wank. Mostly American but a few French chickenish ones too. Are you on the gay scene?"

"No."

"I used to be but the ad keeps me pretty busy—I've given up relying on clubs and my sort of thing is very safe. Do you think you could cope? Strip? You must be warned, the videos are extremely pornographic. You may end up with your balls a lot lighter than when you arrived."

"I'll bring a large box of Kleenex."

"Yes, I couldn't abide my carpet getting spoiled. Wish you were here strutting it now mate. I think you're gonna be pretty good by the sounds of it."

I shook him off with a promise to try and drop by his place some time in the evening.

The day of my twenty seventh birthday, the fifteenth of June, the midday meal and I was getting an ugly head-on view of my father. He sat opposite me sweating in the day's vest. Hairy, heavy arms, elbows on the table, knife and fork raised. An exercise in breathing and masticating at the same time, mouth open, he chewed on special offer beef. My mother served him another helping before coaxing a slab of it towards my plate.

Wearing under my jeans the leather jock strap I'd acquired at the start of the day, I watched him butter and salt his potatoes. No one noticed my thick lip. If they had asked I would have said Hamish had given me a nasty peck.

My father and the generations before him had come from a fishing village near Cork, dependent on a sea forever hurt and angry. It was an area prone to occasional mental disorder, common enough for a community turned in upon itself for centuries. A harshness of life that didn't breed optimism but dogmatism, suspicion, aloof superiority, fatalism. People there told meandering ghost stories while awaiting death. (Preferably the death of others.)

My father was a carpenter before he started up his own building business, serving his apprenticeship in a damp shed in Beara Bay where he made a variety of coffins in different sizes. Handy.

I've learned much from my father: the power of neglect, authoritarianism, murderous rages, deceit and good old fashioned hypocrisy. Zooming from one to ten on the temper scale faster than your average Broadmoor resident, a picture of clenched yellow teeth and jutting chin, he believed in exercising his right to pull/push/grip/shake/slap/smack/bully. I knew his rules at an early age and abided by them. The cold silences, the tick of the clock, all silent for the news at six, seven, nine and ten. I knew what happened if a rule was broken. Those huge, hard hands. From children to mother-in-law, against the wall. Whack! Then the lecture shouted at point-blank range. Or shouting the two favourite words from his limited vocabulary: dumb and stupid. Satisfied only when the teardrops started.

My three sisters had an easier time of it. They toed the line. They knew he'd come in handy when it came to loft conversions and the laying of crazy paving.

His slaps had kind of stunned me. I wouldn't know where I was for a while. That in itself could feel almost nice. Warm and tingly. Tranquillising. Not really there or anywhere. Like stretching and yawning, eyes closed, while taking in the fetid air.

One night the bogey man met up with my father as he was staggering towards his car, tore out his larynx and fed it to a stray dog. A frequent fantasy. In another, the whole family was lying on an analyst's couch, staring up at my father who was having to listen to how we felt while he was strapped to the ceiling with ropes, dressed in his Sunday best and gagged with one very large raw potato. I always feared this fantasy might turn on me and he'd piss down on the lot of us or knock the potato out with his tongue and vomit every drop of his insides down.

I hid when I heard him coming. Under beds, behind bushes, curtains, inside cupboards and wardrobes. While I listened to his tirades from the top of the stairs, I learned to exercise bladder control. I prayed that in his sleep or at the pub, he'd choke on his vomit.

Intensive fantasy-filled masturbation was always a relief. I reserved the tears and sulks for piano practice and long walks alone. While they fretted over my school fees, they didn't question why I bed-rocked or why I threw up every

CALL ME

day before school. They had no idea I was being bullied.

I dreaded the school holidays just as much. Being at home. The arrival of my appalling academic reports. The humiliation. With parents who didn't give quality time chat and an au pair from Limburg, I seemed a bit on the slow side. Delayed speech. I didn't understand my class mates. I was talking German before I talked English.

I didn't belong anywhere. Except with the dogs and cats and the fish in the pond at the top of the garden.

Admitting there was a problem might have given them an indication of the nature of their son. I hid from them that I was being called a poof, queer, faggot and all the rest. For years. Even by the teachers. (A big shout to St Benedict's Public School for Catholic Boys, Eton Rise, Ealing.)

Perhaps a hint of my already non-reproductive instincts, was what worried my parents. They were most distressed years later when I revealed that my remaining testicle had not been covered with lead while undergoing the radiotherapy at Barts. They had continued hoping for grandchildren even when I was living with Ray and getting it up the bum. God bless them.

Their only boy. Their reluctant bloody show piece. I sulked and glared when their visitors said how cute I was and what long eyelashes I had. The strain of being their ambassador to the world made me feel like a resident alien.

"So," my father said chewing, "How's work?"

"Rex Features have placed quite a few picture sets lately. One for *Stern*, two for Japanese magazines. And I've just got a commission from *Le Point* on street markets."

Lies, all lies. Had I said I'd just done the cover of *Time* he'd have said, "That's nice." What he wanted to hear was foreign currencies, particularly those with high exchange rates. My mother thought I should be making it with *The Daily Mail* or putting my play-safe teaching degree to good use. I'm a disappointment. I'm a disappointment to myself most days.

While eating, I fought the impulsive desire to smash everything made of glass in that cosy, claustrophobic bungalow. Windows, all three tv screens, hidden bottles, dainty Waterford Glass, picture frames of births, baptisms and marriages—rarely in that order. Glass is a bugger to clear up. The grandchildren would have to be banished for weeks. Glass splinters get everywhere.

"Well, your honour, the defendant's early years were friendless, closed years of postponed promises, unkept favours. Slovenly years, disordered."

But I got through the meal without any obvious discomfort. I sat and listened to the same same same fucking stories. Family: none of my business—nothing to do with me.

When I told them about Ray and me, when I left home to live with him, their symptoms of trauma had been stiff lips and silence. They didn't accept a single invitation to visit. Not once. They hated Ray and he hated them back. His attitude was kind of refreshing. Direct. My mother telephoned lots when Ray finally snuffed it, but neither came to the stupid service. Not that I'd have wanted them to.

"What would you like for Christmas?" my mother asked as I was leaving.

It's mid June, I thought, for Christ's sake!

"My father's funeral would be nice."

"I'll see what I can arrange," she said, giving me a kiss on the cheek, half smiling.

At Mr Strut It's, the video player was on like a tap, pouring out taken for granted porno on a movie-size wall screen in fabulous Dolby Surround. The video was linked up to the hi-fi, drenching us from mounted speakers. He'd covered his carpet with the kind of polythene sheeting decorators use, a neat precaution against stains or bad karma.

I sat on my bike, emptying his fruit bowl in slow, juicy bites. I'd made a rule when carrying my bike into his living room: No touching! Placing three seats around the cramped low-ceilinged room, I told him he could move from one to another but he had to stay in the chosen seat for a minimum of three minutes.

Being given boundaries in his own home he found both humiliating and wonderfully exciting.

At one point a wasp flew in and made for the fruit bowl.

The performance was halted as he (inordinately terrified) swatted the insect to death with a copy of *The Guardian*.

When his seedless grapes, two oranges, a Golden Delicious and an above average sized banana had disappeared though the appropriate orifice, it was time for the laziest striptease ever. Ridiculous, with the bike as some sort of improbable erotic symbol.

Thankfully, he kept his clothes on. Neat circles and squares cut out of his cheap jeans exposed bits of flesh, like he'd been practising shape-cutting exercises aimed at lower ability kids. He rubbed himself every now and then in a most pathetic way. He'd worn the crotch thin. I made him put his hands on his head like a naughty boy for that.

With my eyes closed I could press the *PLAY* button in my head, rewinding recent shaggable glimpses by fruit stalls, at bus stops.

I imagined I was far out of London in a wood, up a tree, wanking off all alone as I'd done for years before Ray came along. I saw a picture of James Dean like that once—up a tree, clutching his dick. Paid by the hour, so the story goes. Amazing what actors get up to when they're resting.

When I opened my eyes I'd shot beyond the protective polythene he'd laid down. I'd sprayed the video, splashed a Californian hunk faking it for the camera to subsidise a paltry allowance. The things a boy has to do to get through college. He clapped when I'd finished my little show piece, though I don't know what Equity would have made of such a performance.

"How did you get that gorgeous love bite? It's fab! I adore love bites. They're so slaggy. Do us a favour and give me one. Go on. It'd freak them out at work."

I began to think of a few things which would freak him out. Not only him, but his neighbours, those colleagues at work, estranged family, the tabloids. The BBC, Sky, CNN and NHK. I said I'd give him a love bite people would talk about if he washed off some of that aftershave first. He toddled off quite happily to soap and splash the vital parts. Ritualistic last minute ablutions he'd mastered great speed in performing.

CALL ME

While he was behind the locked bathroom door, racing to get back to some tactile contact, one of the many illegal videos featuring minors went into my pannier along with a couple of postal orders already made out to *The Pink Paper* and *Gay Times*. Taking just two was hardly greedy: there were whole bunches of coupons for *Boyz* lined up ready to lure others into his den.

As he over-optimistically douched and lubed, I considered two choices: doing him a favour or creeping out while I had the opportunity. When he came in I was lacing up a pair of Dr Marten boots inherited from Ray. I still wore the black leather jock strap from the shithead in Muswell Hill. A surplus of oil covered my body.

"Oh, very nice!" the queen said.

My chest reddened with each deep sniff of poppers. Perhaps I had that shiny black in my eyes that dogs get when they want to screw or when they see something they're desperate to rip apart. All of a sudden he was whispering like a sissy:

"Hey, I don't want no trouble."

How I hate a double negative.

He moved to the windows. When he drew back one of the three sets of curtains he saw that I'd bolted each and every window catch down. He eyed me with pathetic speculation: *What the...?* Something must have begun to pound in his head in that room which had the not unfamiliar stink of a Thermos Night Sauna cabin in Amsterdam or Dublin's Incognito off Aungier Street. He'd only wanted a nice slow quickie as he'd turned the key in the door, letting me in. What had he let himself in for? Even I didn't know.

"You said you wanted a love bite, my lovely. You're gonna get one. Get down there."

Twisting an arm around his back and putting a hand over his mouth was as easy as in the movies. *Nine To Five* by Sheena Easton began to play in the flat below, very loud. I was the only one who smiled at this.

"Hurry up now. The quicker we do this, the quicker I'll be out of here. The more you comply, the fewer the injuries," I said, winking like it was the greatest bit of fun in the world.

His mouth tried to open behind the palm of my hand. He wanted to say something. I kept my fingers shut tight, squeezed against his face, as if super-glued.

"Shut up! Don't talk. Just get down there. Now!"

I released his mouth, gripping his neck for variation.

(Whispering) "Please."

"Shut up! Come on. On the floor."

(Whispering) "I can't while you've got hold of my neck. Oh." (Then faintly) "Help."

"Sh...Sh... Shut up. Keep quiet and you'll be all right."

"Don't undress me, will you?"

"No fear of that, ugly."

"I'm expecting a phone call at ten o'clock," he said.

"I'm scared."

The man lay obediently on the edge of the polythene sheeting. With the rope I'd decided to bring at the last minute, something Ray had used on me once or twice for fun, I tied his wrists to upper femurs. The body felt very warm through the clothing that covered it. Interestingly, his little dick was semi-erect. I did every button of his shirt up to keep his body odour in as much as possible.

"I want to put this in your mouth." (Pause) "Right in."

"No. No way. Can't we . . ."

"I'll slit your throat if you don't shut up."

I kung-fued the creep a few times playfully.

He stared at that pair of stained pink knickers which Janis had searched high and low for before realising her queer little visitor had pinched them. Maybe he caught a whiff of her cunt, a quick smell of the jogger's rectum or the stink of the spunk the garment had wiped off my bedroom mirror the night before as I removed them slowly from a Sainsbury's grocery section plastic bag. Perhaps he was also catching a whiff of organic carrots. I'd like to think so.

"I'm going to put this in your mouth. Keep it in and you'll be alright."

He shook his ginger head from side to side.

"Hush now."

"I've got your number in my diary," he threatened.

"And I've got your life in my hands," I informed him.

(Heavy breathing, sounds of distress, then childishly)
"Oh. Oh."
"Open wide. If you don't..."
"Oh Euan, please."
"Shut up or you'll get a taste of my sewage pipe."
(Laboured breathing)
"Open wide for Euan. Open wide, love."
"What's this for?" he dared ask. So I slapped him.
Finger marks showed quickly.

I think he said, "I can't breathe," when I pushed the
knicks right to the back of his throat. Had I videoed all this,
the Hi-8 cassette later being discovered among the contents
of a brown suitcase kept under my bed, those sounds might
have been described as *muffled* or *indecipherable*.

When I covered his face, his breath misted the clear
polythene and he looked quite angelic, fading into soft focus
by the minute. He now had a fully erect dick. I gave that
tired little organ a firm-to-hard wanking through the denim.
It probably hurt.

Though his attempts at speech should have been
indecipherable, it's amazing what you can pick up just on
rhythm and intonation:

"I do hope you're not going to kill me," he tried to say,
just above the volume of a seductive schoolboy's last
muffled plea.

"Let's pretend I'm a serial killer," I said. "A serial killer
wanting to beat the record. Forget Bundy, Dahmer, Gacy,
Nilsen, Sutcliffe and West...I'm going to be the best!"

That's when the sobbing started. His mind was
rewinding recent reports of queens cut down in their prime,
in their homes, necks slashed. You can never be too careful.

"You have potential, as a statistic. Ooh you're lovely.
Give us a kiss."

As his life flashed before him, which must have made
tedious viewing, he pulled the face of an ugly cartoon
character who'd just tasted something very hot, making his
mouth open as wide as possible. I spat into it.

That's when he pissed himself, spoiling the carpet,
howling "Nnnggahnoo!" (Followed by a gurgling noise.)

"Try not to be so overtly feeble. What would your poor mother think? Shurrup crying."

The thumb of my right hand pierced the thin polythene. I plucked Janis' sale item out and entered his mouth, feeling the hot, high roof. He gasped like a bad actor in a Crimewatch UK reconstruction. Then he blinked, like he was about to say something, but he didn't. Sheena finished the final chorus downstairs. As the song faded he gulped for air.

He was absolutely silent, just like I used to be when on the receiving end of a thrashing from my father.

He wondered if it was all over. He'd come in his pants, loneliness and despair jutting out on his face in the seconds in which he ejaculated. He'd also, without a doubt now, shat in them. So much for the prolonged douching.

I pictured the piano falling down in slow motion on to him as the clock ticked by. Yawning, I decided against it. I've always been very considerate towards neighbours.

"Thank you," he said. "That was really lovely."

As I knelt beside him, his body odours were no longer concealed by aftershave. His face and neck were wet with sweat. I gnawed at the jugular. "Nnnggahnoo," was the sound he chose to repeat.

Spitting faint traces of blood back into the body, aiming for the back of the throat, I missed. He squeezed both eyes shut like it was acid.

Gargling for safety's sake with a drop of gin from the bottle he'd offered when I arrived, probably laced with sleeping pills (you can never be too careful), I sprayed his carpet with gin. Then I untied the knots Ray had taught me, cheerful as a Blue Peter presenter.

"There now. Tell them at work how you let strangers come knocking at your door, show them your slaggy neck. That'll freak 'em out, duckie!"

He failed the attitude test by sneering just a little from the recovery position he'd assumed on the carpet as Bike Boy waved bye bye, so I took the shiny, sharp knife from my bag and placed it on his bottom lip.

His "Nnnggahnoo," was so much better articulated than before. God is great, He provides for all.

Somewhere close to midnight when the Goswell Road was having one of its quiet moments, Cuddles the teddy bear jumped from the seventh floor, followed by the flowers and that nasty piece of wicker.

No greeting.
This card is blank inside and suitable for all occasions.
No natural forests were destroyed to make this product.
Only farmed timber was used and re-planted.
We hope you enjoy sending this card.
Price code F.
Made in England.

Some illustrator who'd served time on an art course somewhere had done a bread-and-butter graphic of a huge, inflated teddy bear holding a red rose.

For someone special was written in creamy yellow on white.

In the vast, blank interior of the card *D* was initialled inside in angular black, as per usual.

What he wanted were rights of tenure.

"Frank's such a butch name."

"You think so, huh?"

"You've got a nice voice. Bet you've got a nice cock, too."

"I'm not saying it's enormous or anything, but when I push it in all the way...I've been told it hurts."

"Ooh. I think you're going to have to come over. I'll arrange one of my little parties, get the girls round."

Shutting all three sets of curtains which she'd run up herself, Glenda eyed me with adventurous speculation, as did her two friends, also dragged up to the nines: *Will we get those shorts off?* The copulating rhythm was slow to start pounding in that room which had the atmosphere of a surprise party and the stink of a perfume department. While Sarah turned the key in the door, as Bobbie lowered the dimmer switches, Glenda crossed her legs and smiled, showing a crooked line of lipstick over capped front teeth.

"I do hope you're going to be gentle with me, ladies," I whispered.

They'd already got through quite a bit of vodka by the time I got there. A four speed electric fan did its best to keep us all cool. Walking through the door in Dr Martens, cycle shorts and a teeshirt with I CAN FLY on it, shiny silver capitals on black, screams of excitement were to be heard all over Fulham. They took an above average instant interest in the size of my dick and how I came to possess such a gorgeous love bite. When I blushed they all agreed I was such an improvement on that last one and we all wondered where my ejaculate would end up.

All three of them lit candles around the room. Bobbie and Glenda were skinny as rakes and expensively dolled up. I was probably older than Bobbie and Sarah. Glenda was pushing thirty. The flat was an above average nine-to-five torture chamber for City gents.

Watching Jeff Stryker jerk off in a shower, four faces inches from the screen, big fat joint doing the rounds, I felt pleasantly relaxed. When Glenda ran a hand over my legs she shrieked and turned up the lights for a better look.

"Right girls! Louis Marcel to the rescue!"

"You don't want to shave yer lallies luv," said Sarah. "Waxing's best. One treatment removes unwanted hair for up to six weeks."

"Ooh, you sound like the side of the box Sarah. Give us a strip of the stuff and hold him down. He's wriggling."

Glenda sprinkled talc below my left knee. I gave up the pretence of being an unwilling victim and allowed them to have their wicked way. Glenda blew off the excess powder. The strip was cut in half, backing sheet removed, then pressed firmly on the skin in the direction of hair growth.

"Darlings," Bobbie announced. "This isn't going to work. Is that unsightly stubble a minimum of four millimetres long? I ask you!"

Holding the skin taut with one hand, Glenda pulled the strip back on itself very quickly in the opposite direction to hair growth. Ninety nine per cent of the stubble stayed firm.

"We're going to have to shave him!" Sarah squealed.

"Oh, please!" said Bobbie. "Can't we have a drink first?"

Glenda gave me the rest of the strips, advising me to keep them in the fridge. She didn't need them, she'd progressed to proper waxing at a salon.

The cocaine was chopped for a good five minutes. We each took a line through a tenner. Sarah coughed, bloodshot eyes needing an extensive retouch. I opened a bottle of champagne stolen from a press launch at Lynne Franks a couple of months back. Nasty stuff, much appreciated.

A fly came into the room and Glenda spotted it instantly. It made a big mistake, huge, by aiming for Jeff Stryker. Fake nails flashed through the air, dragging the juicy debris over the screen as Stryker delivered a million dollar mumble, shooting his muck. We all tittered.

"Flies, dirty things. Hate 'em," Glenda pronounced, sucking her drink down sharply. "They spread germs."

"I detest bugs. How dare they enter my little nest without permission?" Bobbie joined in. "I don't like to kill them. What I normally do is put a glass over them, then they just die. That way it's not like *I* killed them."

A sharing moment.

"There's a woman trapped inside this body," Sarah whispered to me in an awkward silence. The new Take That release had come to an end.

"Well dear," Glenda sneered, panto-style, raising a plucked and pencilled eyebrow, "...judging by the shape of you the woman trapped inside is heavily pregnant."

This had all been said before and no offence was taken. They were putting on a little show for me. It only seemed fair to do likewise. Pretending to be hot I removed my teeshirt. Sarah put a variety of simple, thumping, computer pop CDs on random select while Glenda headed off towards the bathroom.

"You could make a lot of money with a body like yours. Modelling," said Bobbie while adding gloss to a mouth already heavily lipsticked.

"Or whoring," Sarah said, more to the tv screen than me, like it was a reasonable option for any young man. (Which it is.)

The second line of cocaine quietened all of us as my naked body was shaved. It was so nice. Three GII blades dragging along slowly. Sarah Immac-ed my armpits considerately, not wanting to scrape in the semi-darkness. Bobbie took charge of my groin, applying shaving foam only after a very slow tongue bath. Glenda was matter of fact with the larger expanses of flesh. When I was turned over my arse was hers.

Her tongue licked long and slow and deep. So warm, so wet, so softly. Her breath entered my body, blowing my bowels up like a balloon, easing me into doggy position, repeating the cycle of long, slow, deep rimming, developing into a penetration softer than a dick and so much more pleasurable in its delicacy.

One of them said, "I'm putting on a condom, alright?"

And I said, "Yeah." I was so stoned I couldn't have moved if the place was on fire.

Left alone for maybe as long as thirty minutes, I drank more than half a bottle of Vodka. By the phone lay a pile of those lurid kinky cards you see in phone booths. Dragging a wet finger over the mirror, catching the last of the cocaine to spread over my gums, I was well out of it by the time they returned dressed in see-through nighties.

It was like the bathroom was on fire. Candles on all levels flickered through the steam. The water was warm to hot. They put me in the bath to soak, then took it in turns to attend to my body. Sarah washed my cropped head softly, rinsing more carefully than a midwife. The gentle, stroking combing of my eyebrows and eyelashes was sweet. Her tongue licked my lips in a sideways figure of eight, over and over.

Glenda sang a rugby song, circling my nipples with a red-glossed nail.

Bobbie sat watching for a long while before a manicure which gave me the shivers.

Hold me down, I thought. Hold me down under these shiny silvery bubbles. No one knows where I am. No one cares, certainly not me.

"You're a very beautiful young man," Bobbie whispered.

Tears came to my eyes. Of all the things in the whole, narrow-minded world, I was thinking of a scrawny green budgie named Hamish.

Once towelled by all three sisters, I was tied to a post in another room, empty but for one red bulb.

Through half-closed eyes Glenda put on a generous amount of dark red Avon lipstick and placed a slow, soft kiss over my pumping heart. Bobbie followed, lips brimming with Chanel pink and placed two lipstick kisses on my neck, transforming the foul love bite. Sarah busied herself with a purple by Shiseido, leaving imprints above my navel, right nipple and forehead. They all reapplied with equal generosity, with staggered timing, each having a fair share of their captive human canvas. Soon every inch of my body was covered with lipstick kisses.

"Put a record on," I demanded of anyone.

Somebody did me the favour. It was the Blur single I'd had in my head since the time with the boy by the bins.

The colour at the base of my penis was dark red. Fuschia, I suppose. Thoughtful improvements to neck, bite and scar on the lower left abdomen were a candyish pink. Lips and eyes purple. Probably colours with exotic names like 'Sheer Midnight'.

Along the King's Road and through Hyde Park to turn heads in Piccadilly, I pedalled smooth, muscular legs covered with lipstick marks like bullet holes.

A light shower around 4am brought dust and pollen down, improving the air quality. The Goswell Road was quiet.

I found a postcard in my pannier, a picture of the Royal Family. On the back was a telephone number and Glenda's signature in large, right slanting loops. More interestingly, a neatly folded fifty pound note plus a small transparent plastic sachet of white powder sellotaped to the corner. From the mouth of Queen Elizabeth II came a speech bubble: 'Hope to see you again!'

It was great to return to a blank answerphone. Unplugging that and the phone was a new claim on my right to silence. I was tired of raspberries, silly little messages and hopeful voices leaving numbers twice in their best voice and manners. And Dai's late-night, long-distance static, crackle, grit and tell-tale pips.

Opening the balcony door to check that Hamish was in his cage, I remembered Jessie was back and Hamish had gone. I kind of laughed to myself about how I'd cried only yesterday, or the day before. Whenever. Birds were already singing but not my Hamish. It was dawn.

I did the cocaine then switched on. When the DRUMS voice was selected (voice number ninety nine), twenty five different drum and percussion instruments could be played on the black keys. I mainly used the same sounds:

C#1...Bass Drum Reverb
D#1...Bass Drum
G#1...Lo Tom
D#2...Snare Reverb
C#.....Snare Closed Rim
F#3...Hi-Hat Open
A#3...Crash
C#4...Splash Cymbal
D#4...Ride Cymbal

The accompaniment was very well behaved. Pressing the SYNCHRO START/ENDING button started the accompaniment off perfectly every time I played the first note on the keyboard. The three red dots along the bottom of the MULTI DISPLAY flashed at the selected tempo, helping me keep time.

The left side of my face often looked bruised after I'd been behind my Yamaha for an hour or two. I leaned that side of my head heavily on my left arm, fingering the keys in SINGLE FINGER mode.

I missed Hamish landing on my head, chewing the cord, banging his beak against the headphones. I wrote 'Invasion Of The Dark Kisses' on the cassette label, then slept. In the morning red, brown and deep purple clotted the sheets.

Jessie came knocking around nine, but I couldn't open the door, not looking like the 'After' in a belt up campaign. I could see another delivery had come. I crept into the bathroom to have my second long soak of the day.

Jessie came knocking again at noon.

"These came for you yesterday, round five, you were out. Aren't they lovely? What it is to be popular!"

"How's Hamish?"

"Oh, fine. You okay? You're a bit purple around the eyes."

I sniffed a bit and smiled.

"Bloody hayfever's doing me in!" I said sweetly. She looked at the black polo neck I was wearing, dressed far too warmly for the day.

Dai had sent another wicker basket, this time with a dainty handle and housing four little plants. 'Summer Delights'. They'd sweated in polythene overnight.

D.

Placing the basket on the floor of the lift, I waved goodbye to it as the doors shut and the lift was called to the fourteenth floor.

"Hello. Is that 0171 608 ——? Roger?"

I was taken aback by the ancient tones of another era.

"Uh-huh."

"Ah. I've had this note from you in response to an ad I think I had in *Capital Gay*. Is that right and you are Roger?"

"Yes, I replied!"

"To my ad!"

"For one-legged guys!"

"That I wanted to meet one. My name is Glancey, the Christian name is Gerald."

"Gerald Glancey."

"Well, Gerald is one of my names. Actually it's Henry. My little code system. So I know, you know. Well, I've had this kink, if you can call it so, all my life. I'm attracted to one-legged guys, amputees. I wonder, are you an amputee?"

"No, fortunately I've got both. Sorry!"

"No, don't apologise. It's a good thing, for you... unfortunate for moi. Are you inclined towards amputees?"

"I've never admitted this to anyone before, always felt kind of ashamed of it. Tried not to think of it even."

(Pause.)

"Go on."

"A couple of years ago, I saw this boy my age at Trade, a queer club round the corner from where I live. Really cute he was, too. Fancied him rotten."

"Oh yes?"

"Young boy, blond boy, sexy boy."

(Like the start of an ad.)

"Mmm. Continue."

"I sat and watched him dance, a bouncing head amongst the crowd."

"Dancing, yes."

"Then I spotted he was Thalidomide. He had these stumpy arms. I found him more attractive when I discovered that. I don't know. Maybe it's a domination thing. I really don't know, just don't understand myself. Well, when I saw your ad I thought maybe you'd understand. Do you understand? I'm frightened of this fascination. But, secretly, Henry, I love every minute of it."

This was punctuated by the occasional sniff. He thought I was getting all emotional. It was, of course, the after-effect of a night in with the girls.

"I see," he said, slowly.

"We've got a kind of...similar sort of...interest."

"Except yours is arms. You are interested in amputated arms, or the lack of them. With me it's legs. You're obviously very young."

"Twenty one, just recently."

"Knew it, could tell by your voice. Well, if you'd like to talk to me I'm always here. You must understand that you are not a pervert. Lots of people have kinks. I like one-legged guys. Simple. I know a doctor who does. It doesn't mean you're insane. Enjoy it!" (Pause) "I belong to the British Amputee Sports Association. They have a sports day at Stoke Mandeville Hospital every year. There are people doing all sorts of things, high jumps and all sorts. Last year the weather was perfect, everyone stripped off. We're going on the last Saturday of June, a one-legged friend and myself. Would you like to come along?"

"Sounds very exciting, Henry."

"Oh, it is. I get very excited by amputees, their hopping about. I want an affair with one. It's lovely speaking to you Roger... Are you normal otherwise? Do you go with girls?"

"No. Queer as fuck, your honour."

"I'm very pleased to hear that. Women can't be trusted, you know. Turn your back for a moment and they're soaking their knickers in the bidet. You sound nice and butch. Are you well-endowed? You know, I'm only asking."

I didn't answer. A number of options came to mind at this point: he was getting a hard-on/had a hard-on and was getting playful/was into a full-scale wank and looking for something absorbent to come on.

"Are you nice looking?" said in a horror film whisper.

"I'm just a normal boy, really."

The telephone manner of a future well-heeled hooker.

"Do you wear glasses?"

"Not yet."

"I'm just trying to get a picture of you, Roger. You see...I live quite alone. I know lots of people. I was visiting friends in the country only yesterday. I'm not a person who'd take advantage of you in any way. So, how's about getting your young arse round as soon as possible then?" (Laughs) "Or would you feel it was like walking into a lion's den? Promise not to gobble you up, unless you want me to!" (Pause.) "I'm in Islington, North London. N1."

"Really? That's close. I live near Angel tube."

"Walking distance, even with one leg. Just a hop and a skip away," the old fuck said. He laughed alone. "I'm behind Camden Passage, Duncan Terrace. Just off Upper Street."

"I know it, off Colebrooke Row, near the Orton and Halliwell residence."

"Ah, yes. It's become quite a queer landmark has that."

I stopped off at Chapel Market on the way. There's this barrow boy on the corner, absolutely skeletal—pale as a ghost. Works on the fruit stall outside Marks & Spencers. He's that sexy anything age between sixteen and nineteen. A reformed Geordie layabout in a baseball cap who always asks if I'm "Alright?" Bleary-eyed on Sunday mornings from being up all night. I'd like to cut that down-to-his-arse hair off while he's sleeping. And it's—naturally—an arse to die for in tight, faded Levi's: firm young buttocks nicely lifted and separated. Cool, white, marvellously rounded, just the way I like them. A Steve or Adam, Spencer or Jason. "Anything else?" he always asks with the cheekiest smile on his face. Gorgeous...Straight as anything, of course.

When he saw me leaning against the wall, waiting for the front door of the basement flat to open, my right leg tucked up under my knee, the old boy thought he had a legless lovely before him for one sweet second. There was a beat in which he looked me over, from Blondie teeshirt to ankles.

"You've got a nice pair of legs, Roger. Shame you've got two of them."

Henry. God had a wild time making the mould for that one's face. He had one of those big ugly heads that you get sitting right in front of you at the cinema. This head was mounted on the neck of an aging labrador. Nose hairs you could make tooth-brushes out of. He was breathless, seventy seven and smelly.

As he let me in his eyes savoured the fading love bite while his nose sniffed the ripe pineapple I handed him.

He'd lived a full life down in that basement. The kitchen area had something, somewhere that stank. It might have come from the towels, floorboards or drains. Perhaps a combination. Whatever, wherever, it needed sorting out.

Henry didn't sit but fell backwards into the chair, looking like a fresh delivery to Casualty. He'd worked hard paying contributions towards the National Health Service and now it had let him down.

Punctuating the mantelpiece were postcards, many from Greece. They all featured remnants of human shapes in stone. I could imagine him circling long, cool halls, caressing the collections of Greek statuary, Kouroi artfully placed on pedestals, casting elegant shadows. I bet he'd kissed cool nipples, slid his hands over lovely pale buttocks, fingered the mutilated groins of stony youths.

I wanted the promised coffee but he'd started the tour of Olympia. We'd already visited the Doric temple of Zeus. The pages were marked and ready for staring eyes. He talked in snatches, presuming I knew who and what these sculptures represented.

"Kiadeos, east pediment, ah yes...the river-god, just look at that stretching forth, there's an absolutely armless one for you! Oinomaos, Myrtilos, the kneeling youth, Lapith youth...Oh, that headless, armless, penisless Centaur is mine, if you don't mind. Ha! Take your eyes off him, he's mine! Oh, you'd adore Apollo from The Tiber in El Museo Nazionale delle Terme in Rome. Absolutely stumpy, Roger. I've travelled a bit. I know what I like," he said clutching my right knee.

"There was a report, Roger, of three puritanical shits— English of course—who, when visiting a museum in Athens at the turn of the century, brandished hammers and chisels and chopped off two hundred and thirty one penises and God knows how many pairs of balls before the authorities, two attendants in their seventies in this case, got the situation in hand."

"Ouch!" I said to humour him. While he put the kettle on I inspected torsos, cupids, angels and saints as recommended.

He particularly liked Hermes and the infant Dionysus by Praxiteles in the Olympia Museum. Giving them a once over quietened him down.

"Pass over the Michelangelo like a luv. Now, look at that bum. What do you think of that?"

"Cool, white, marvellously shadowed."

He swallowed audibly.

"Yes. I can see we're going to get on very nicely."

Shutting all three sets of curtains he eyed me with nervous speculation: *Is he from News International?* The copulating rhythm of the universe began to pound as the slide projector shone the torso of Hermes upon the wall by the bed. He'd bought the slides from some museum: Torso of Hermes (many angles), Herakles (side view, front view and rear).

When the slide show had finished, not wanting to raise his considerable bulk from the chair, he simply unscrewed the projector's bulb. The internal fan continued to buzz. Not much light came in from the small back window and no seepage from the curtains.

"I do hope you're going to kill me," I said, at a volume he didn't quite hear.

"Thrill you? Is that what you said? Turn the kettle off dear, while I hunt out some photos my doctor friend popped round. He's a keen photographer and has easy access to amputees. He's got a friend at Guys who...No, turn it to the left. That's right."

Young boys, clinically documented before and after surgery, from many angles. (Side views, front views, lots of rear.) Previous BASA sports days featuring legless youths swimming, hopping the fifty yards, clearing moderate to great heights in the high jump. Male amputees in gleaming wheelchairs, with trophies and vulnerable smiles. Unaware pin-up boys, zoom-ins of crotches on crutches. One amputee had such a dignified face, freckled and alert. He was gorgeous. The missing leg seemed no hindrance to his being. He stood proud, holding himself a little to one side for balance.

"I can see you like that one. Have it. Go on, do. He's yours. My doctor friend won't mind, a bit too grown-up for his liking. Take him. Yours."

"Something for my kitchen wall."

"I'd love to see you fuck him right under my nose," the man said, as he stood to draw back the curtains. "I usually like a leg clean off but sometimes a foot can be very exciting. Cut above the knee is preferable to below. The higher up the more I like it. The stump, I love to rub it where the leg used to be. There's nothing like rubbing a stumpy femur."

The Cadbury's chocolate cake didn't resemble the picture on the box. Like the Elgin Marbles it was cracked and chipped, but still intact here and there. It was served rather like confetti.

"I do like legged men too, only secondary though. Take a look in those drawers," he said, before slurping down his coffee through teeth the colour of a rising full moon.

Years and years of yellowing lovelies he'd dedicated many a wank to, divine pornography awaiting the life-giving inspection. *Q International, Hunk, Colt, Binky, Blueboy.* He had the *Vulcan* I'd seen at Mr Mok's house that featured Ray in various stages of undress long before I'd met him in the Radiotherapy Department of Barts Hospital. Randy Ray.

"Nice dick on that one," he said.

"Not any more."

This card is made of wood pulp from managed forests. For every tree cut down at least one more is replanted, this replenishes Earth's atmosphere.
Price code F.
Made in England.
Writing your own personal message makes this card more special.

I opened the envelope beside the toilet.

The graphic was a tasteful mountain view at sunset, captured inspiringly in golds and reds, carefully costed in terms of ink. Hazy geese flying lazily, free from acid rain. A narrow grey road zigzagged the rock face.

Printed in elaborate italics below the graphic:
I've searched high and low for a friend like you...
Inside, in capital letters, Dai had written:
Gotcha!
D

Both card and envelope were neatly torn into precise squares, then, with one quick flick of the wrist, flushed away in an instant.

Stoke Mandeville hovered in the diary. I babysat the idea with the occasional phone call.

Alfred, an amputee cut high at the left, struck me as a very cool sort of chap. At his stage in life he had an objective view, the storyline of his life was clear. There'd be no happy ending, just his part-time job, sleep, pornography and paid boys trying to remember their fake names.

The road to Aylesbury was smooth. Alfred drove the blue Ford Escort at a sedate pace. Urinals and lock-ups containing the bowls of Twyfords, Civic and Armitage Shanks figured large in the conversation on the way.

"Used to get these awful sore throats," Henry said, "such a pity all those pissoirs are now closed down."

"Sauna's the thing now if you want a bit of fun, unless you're prepared to part with fifty quid should a cutie come your way," said Alfred, making smiling eye contact in the rear-view mirror. "Brownies, 309 and Starsteam are all pretty good, but you can't beat York Hall. You'll have to go there some time. Make the most of your genitals while you're young!" he said with a wink.

Small queer world.

"We met in Greenwich Baths way back after the war," Alfred continued.

"Best shilling a man could spend," said Henry. "I saw Alfred hopping about in there and tossed him off."

"Place was a bit slippy," said Alfred.

"York Hall is every Tuesday, Thursday and Saturday. I'm not sure if it's women on a Friday. I think it's changed since they painted the place yellow," Henry said.

"It's behind the old town hall, next to the toy museum or whatever it is. Two-minute walk from Bethnal Green tube. Best wank in London." Alfred laughed, dragging a tongue over lips which had done mileage.

I lost count of legs off in car crashes, motor-bike accidents, misadventures on the factory floor. Limbs crushed, ripped, torn away, pulled clean off for ever. Born without, born deformed, some like curly pasta. God knows best. God moves in some pretty mysterious ways. God placed the doctor friend beside me to give medical histories and prick lengths.

"There are a lot of fresh little ones about. Just look at the bottom on that one! Oh, I do love to see them hop!"

Prosthetics squeaked in the one hundred metres towards a finishing line grey with salivating men behind cameras. Crutches versus wheel-chairs, legless versus armless. I was introduced all day long to people into humps, bumps, lumps and stumps. A cheerful man named Simon Wright handled last year's snaps with the formality of a magistrate perusing evidence seized at the scene of the crime. He winked, passing an A5 price list promising a same day service.

"Broke his leg in eight places in some sort of pile up a few years back and, so the story goes," Alfred whispered, "became very interested in legs and things. Got initiated by the chap in the next bed one night, an amputee. He'll bore you for hours about four-point knee braces, myoelectric cosmetic gloves, electric elbows, all things to do with orthopaedics and prosthetics. He's not averse to a couple o' slices of fish on his plate either. Loves women in silicone skin coverings, on the legs, so word has it. Really into being jerked off with switch-controlled prosthetic hands. I'd be scared myself, don't know what the voltage could do and the grip on those things can be erratic. Just imagine!"

As the shot-put got under way, a creature from Crawley arrived hot and bothered at being late, carrying one very long telephoto lens and a pair of binoculars. He cruised the toilets all day long: toilets by the playing fields, cafe, canteen, badminton courts, bar and dormitories. Prolonged haunting of the table-tennis area, where the juniors skulked waiting for the swimming to start, got the attention of some parents. I later heard he actually ran a pet shop.

He was very pleased to meet me, but would have preferred me mutilated. Said he'd do me a discount for a budgie with cage and accessories if I continued to miss wee Hamish. Had he been on my shoulder, Hamish would have told the creep to piss off.

It was humid and evaporating chlorine stung my eyes. More and more numb as the day went on, I kept noticing a pretty girl hugging and encouraging her limbless lover who came second to last in every event. I envied their closeness. It made me feel so inadequate.

There was a tremendous surge of animation by the pool-side:

"Had a raging hard-on during the weight-lifting," Henry shouted across to Alfred who blinked his dyed lashes and looked away.

"With me it was the high jump. That boy with the arm off was pretty good, but the one who came second was a little smasher. A very high amputation."

"Yes," said Henry, "worth fifteen minutes of anybody's time!"

"Good job you had your mac on," Alfred said quietly, still looking away.

"A mac with such deep pockets!" someone said too loudly.

Beside the group of amputee enthusiasts plus one voyeur, a family sat waiting for the swimming to start. Their fifteen-year-old son's first sporting day since the op' two years back. Henry was unaware of his volume, or didn't care. The family glared, then moved away.

"See that one there, with the blue towel? Leg off in the Falklands my doctor friend tells me. Mar-vellous! Hung like a donkey by all accounts." Henry smiled like a madman.

There, waiting his turn in the next race, stood the guy I had the picture of. Henry had forgotten that. Close up he was much taller than I'd have thought. He smiled at me, nervous at the prospect of competition.

"Good luck," I said.

Most of the competitors didn't dive but fell into the water. The starter knew how to handle the situation, shouting a quick 'Starting position, swimmers', then bang! Gunshot. Before anyone could lose balance or wobble.

There was front crawl with one arm. Armless backstroke. Breaststroke with no legs—no chance of being disqualified for a screw kick there. One armed butterfly. It was a well organised event. A joy for participants, interesting for parents, fascinating for a chosen few.

A1 *Double above knee*
A2 *Single above knee*
A3 *Double below knee*
A4 *Single below knee*
A5 *Double above elbow*
A6 *Single above elbow*
A7 *Double below elbow*
A8 *Single below elbow*
A9 *Combined lower limb plus upper limb amputation*

Those zoom lenses got busy. They had to be frequently wiped down, with the steam coming off so many warm, wet bodies. The copulating rhythm of the universe began to pound in the spectators' section. Chlorine camouflaged a variety of unpleasant body odours. Henry's doctor friend was busy at the pool-side with a video camera of broadcast quality and a number of still cameras set on *AUTO*.

The doctor waved to Henry, flashing me his vile, delicate, pederast's smile. I gave him a vile, delicate smile back. His face changed. If anyone got the feeling that there was an outsider on the inside, it was that doctor who sniffed me out.

ABSOLUTELY

Once a week a body is found in The Thames, fifty one last year. Most are down and outs no longer able to cope with care in the community. I was sure Dai had an impressive heap of psychiatric problems tucked away in a file somewhere. I was beginning to wish he'd become a Thames statistic.

Attached to the pretty little floral display of creams, yellows and pinks against a background of fern leaves, a box contained three hand-made chocolates.

The envelope, unopened, sailed down the chute. I didn't want to see the solitary *D*.

An admirable economy of words was waiting for me among the late-night, long distance static, crackle and grit, breathing, pips, faint background noise, exhalations, more pips and slammed-down receivers, raspberries, and well mannered voices repeating their number twice.

"You'll have your little shaved balls cut off and force fed down that lovely throat of yours one of these fine days, after they've been fried in dog's piss first, of course."

What it is to have admirers. What it is to have an answerphone. Good job I didn't have a fax.

Bad thoughts approached stealthily like fog invading fields. Unhurried and regular, to the beat of my pulse.

To avoid that dreaded morning feeling I rose at two. Even that took some self-coaxing. I was sick and tired of how big the bed was still without Ray, of the sadness like a virus I couldn't quite shake off.

With a sighing effort I plugged in the tv, switching on trash starring Cary Grant. I sat, wrapped in the duvet. It was cold for July. The film was 'The Bishop's Wife'. There was a hot, sore feeling at the pit of my stomach, the focal point of my depression. Thought was difficult. I'd withdrawn into myself so much that I couldn't follow the dialogue.

After the day at Stoke Mandeville, I called a halt on my project. I didn't want to meet kooky characters any more. Both telephone and answerphone took a rest. Having no desire to go out, I stayed in, wondering what I could do— where I could go.

Somewhere in the UK there's a paint factory, opened circa 1953, producing colours exclusively for prisons, bingo halls and municipal leisure facilities. Dull greens, sighing blues, insipid creams and greys. A good proportion of that factory's sorry output has ended up on the walls of York Hall in Bethnal Green. It's a thick smell down there: distilled stale sweat, infected hawked phlegm, anti-dandruff shampoo, farts from unsavoury buttocks, urine and stale popcorn; which suits the colour scheme of yellow and white. A rank, ruttish stench of spermatozoa uselessly flagellating tails as they die down the drains of a subterranean kingdom.

Since 1929 it's been home to many a fungal infection and sexual compulsive in search of a bit of fun. It's a place of lazy camaraderie: substandard off-the-rack bodies, their purple veins swelled to bursting, exchange weary smalltalk within sub-ecclesiastical architecture designed to encourage hush. The Krays used to go there. Michael Cashman, too.

Eyes in half-familiar faces seemed especially alert to a newcomer; with the grey institutional towel wrapped around my waist, I became my cock, the curve of my arse, pecs, waist, weight. Through interconnecting catacombs and chambers floored in chequerboard stone and walled in the glazed white tiling common to corrective and sanitary institutions of that era, I was followed by a handsome Asian youth. Hot room, steam room, showers, tiled bath the size and depth of a cattle dip, sauna.

"Kuldip."

A simple answer to a simple question.

"Kuldip," he repeated, probably out of surprise at being asked his name. The mutual fumbling in the toilet took only a couple of minutes. He'd started playing with his dick the minute we were alone in the sauna, only stopping briefly when a fat old queen with a sulky cock came in, continuing until another entered, brazen enough to try and get involved. It took no more than a wink for me to follow him to the cold, slippery-floored toilets.

"We gotta be quick," he said, closing the cubicle door.

On rolling back his foreskin, Stilton came to mind, but I still thrust my tongue deep into his mouth. I don't think he wanted to be kissed (he'd probably got a little lady and two kids tucked away somewhere) but it was while I snogged him so forcibly that a minigalaxy of sperm shot from his long, thin dick.

Back in the steam room, mutual discarding achieved over a shared can of Tango, I had the feeling I was on the wrong train and it was time to get off. There was still time to jump, I thought, take a holiday, rustle up a couple of travel features. Maybe I could sweet talk *Chat*. After a while I realised my ears were stinging.

Cooling down under a shower, I was aware of each and every white haired old man, their skins bleached from hours of ambling about in the wet. I could almost hear their lunches sluice through their guts. Here queens rubbed shoulders with villains, cab drivers and tradesmen, all after a touch of the vapours. Made equal by the steam. Boxers go, supposedly, to lose their bruises, taxi drivers their lumbago. Theatrical types to maintain their instrument. The majority looked singularly miserable as they loitered with intent.

Taking a breather between orgasms, two slightly younger but also white haired men sitting on grey plastic chairs, Sunday-in-Broadstairs, pointed me out to each other. I recognised the one on the left. His woolly pendulous torso adorned my kitchen wall like an imaginary beast from a Salvador Dali painting. What, I tried to remember, was he into? I smiled, turning my back, giving them a bit of arse to savour.

Another, breaking the boredom of loitering by taking occasional sips from the water fountain, followed me into the steam room after I'd finished showering.

"Fancy a rub?" he asked all chummy, placing a paw between my shoulder-blades.

"Okay," was the simple go signal he'd been hoping for, pitched an octave lower than usual.

While I lay on a slab of grey marble, delicate hands lathered and kneaded my body with matronly attention, occasionally giving my flaccid prick a rub-down to see if an erection were on the go. When he realised that he wasn't going to have something hard to suck on, he rinsed me off with a bucket of cold water rather abruptly, patted me on the bottom twice to show there were no hard feelings, then left whistling like a sailor.

Moving to the far corner of the empty steam room, I sat cross legged in the corner and began to jerk off, invisible in the steam. The door squeaked.

There was an inrush of light and cool air. Wondering if the sound of my wet foreskin rolling back and forth could be heard, I stopped abruptly. Slow footsteps came my way. A dark silhouette stood before me.

"Hello Bike Boy," the silhouette said, taking a seat beside me on the marble shelf, placing a hand on my right knee. "You walked right past me in the changing rooms."

My erection deflated in an instant. The accent struck a chord, faintly. His dark eyes drew mine for a full ten seconds. When I heard the smoker's cough I knew who it was: Jack from Hampstead.

"I liked those photos you took of me," he said, raising a hand to my right nipple. Perhaps he detected an increase in size since he'd last played with them.

That'll teach you for falling asleep with a stranger," I said, my voice pitched an octave higher than usual, trying to sound boyish, just a bit scared to tell the truth. We both laughed at this as he put his hands around my neck.

"In today's high speed world we all, by varying degrees, leave behind a trail of debris in our frissive interactions with others: lovers, friends—"

"And victims," I interrupted.

"And victims," he echoed.

He began to squeeze those hands around my neck, increasing pressure very slowly, face closing in on mine. His towel slipped off him as he crouched over me on the bench. As we kissed, my air supply was cut off. I didn't struggle. I felt very calm, closing my eyes, going limp. Then he let go. He laughed a little as if it was the biggest joke, which maybe it was. He slapped my face playfully, just the once. It was so soft, welcome.

It must be getting dark outside, I thought as he got down on his knees to pogo his head. I was hard in his mouth in seconds. But it's never really dark in a city, not black black, except under pillows, floorboards and mud, under the influence of drink, behind a shiny leather mask, deep in a drug-induced sleep in bricked up cellars. He tossed me off, tonguing my ear, looking me over as I made a silent donation directly into the sperm bank drain.

I wasn't looking forward to the fifteen-minute ride through miserable Bethnal Green sidestreets strung with second-hand cars. I dreaded rewinding the answerphone in Ray's old home, the raspberries and the pips. There are lots of other people in this world besides Mr Right.

"Want to come back to my place?" is what I wanted the man with the smoker's cough to ask. "Don't see why not," would've been my answer. He didn't pop the question. We showered side by side in silence.

"Take care," was what he said without looking at me, as I rinsed the bubbles off after a soaping I didn't need.

The paper used for the production of this card comes from a sustained forest.
This card is blank for your special message.
Price Code F
Made and printed in England.
D

The mad Welshman had sent a gouache of six blurred boys, cycling down a hill. Rear view. I considered wiping my arse with it and returning to sender.

"Whoever it is must be serious," Jessie said, handing me a slender white box tightly tied with a red ribbon, smiling less this time and not winking as she shut her door.

A sprig of baby's breath had protected the single red rose in transit. Those petals fell one at a time as I stood over the toilet, whispering to the bowl, *He loves me, he loves me not.*

Imagining his face being punched by a freckled fist lightened my mood. I'd reduced the situation to a pseudo-shocked vaudeville act.

Pausing over the bowl, now polka-dotted red, I varied the words: *He is insane, he's not insane, he is insane, he's not insane. He's going to kill me, he's not going to kill me, he's going to kill me, he's not going to kill me.*

Through the open window I heard Hamish. I strained to hear his song. When the phone rang I jumped, then flushed.

Lifting the receiver all I heard was long-distance static. No words. Pip.

The hours I've spent, the energy I've used in the search for symmetry: countless. When the sparks start flying in my brain, off I go with the hoover. Spontaneous, frantic. It's like a hiccup of the mind. Vacuuming until it feels right. I need these rituals for the moments of peace they can offer. What I really want is not to need them. Different compulsions surface when I leave my front door.

It was close to dark when the little itch began. The bell in my head went *ding* and I thought mmm mmm— something's going to happen tonight.

I was dying for it. Thought my prick would burst, the skin was stretched so tight. I couldn't stand being in. So close and muggy. I couldn't breathe. The Beaufort Scale was on zero. My heart was beating itself to death waiting for the storm to break. Sniffing the air and looking upwards I could feel it coming and I wanted to be there, in it.

I was barely conscious, yet perfect in motion. In nothing but my shorts and racing shoes, minus ankle socks, I walked out and rode off.

When the rain fell it was lovely. My nipples hardened in the breeze as I went down the hill from Angel towards Kings Cross in the last of the bright, flat light before the storm. I was cycling without direction, yet knowing where to make each turn, taking the short cuts through Camden, moving in darkness without lights. Sometimes a bike just takes you where you want to go.

Behind Jack Straw's Castle, under a warlike sky, London's mutual masturbators welcomed me to their dark, secret club. The glowing butts of cigarettes hovered and floated in the darkness more like tropical insects than votive candles. Faceless fucks with hard-ons for death, in silent slow-motion walking round and round in circles, stamping

down the growing green. Bachelor ramblers begging to get
their heads kicked in. Keats walked on it, Constable painted
it. At different times the Heath offers something to
everyone. From the Royal Artillery cooling off their horses
to champion boxers in training for a match. Once a refuge
for people suffering from the Great Plague of London; in
that respect it has not changed.

Morning constitutionals are often interrupted by the
sight of condoms and rubber gloves hanging from branches.
The Heath's a twenty four hour free-for-all and a graveyard
of sweet memories. Everything goes on there, every sexual
excess of which flesh is capable. Enter AYOR. No admission
fee. Kamikaze queers more than welcome.

The cold dark edges invited me in, joining the herd busy
digging graves with their cocks. Cold dark edges insisted I
enter to belong in the dark. Grinding round the interior of
my skull was a tune I'd made up the day before. Loathsome,
slow notes. Circling.

Though it was dark I could see a dummy getting fisted.
His eyes were focused on nowhere as his arse took it,
moaning as the fingers explored, coming alive like a glove
puppet once each finger had wriggled deep inside his tubing.

I pushed my bike along with a lazy, hip swaying thrust,
hunting a five minute friend, playing lunatic hide-and-seek.
After walking round, aware that my quality control barrier
was slipping every ten paces, I made the random selection of
a buck-toothed, nipple-pierced baldy ready for anything on
bended knees. His left hand slid up through the back of my
shorts as his mouth warmed my cock inch by inch,
providing mouth-to-dick resuscitation. While the thumb of
his right hand did a fair rotation up my arse, my dick bashed
the candida deep in his throat. No sub-text. No foreplay. As
the thumb poked deeper, I neared orgasm.

Withdrawing his hand from the warmth of my shorts, he
began to suck on the baby turd he'd harpooned with his
thumb. Another dead-alive, catching a whiff of fresh shit,
perhaps jealous of the brown dug out of pale flesh,
approached quickly and stood close.

I could have been stabbed, or raped. I could have been

CALL ME

so very very dead. Heart cut out and hung from a tree for birds to pick at, flies to vomit over, suck up, lay shiny eggs upon...Yes, I might have known agonizing pain for seconds. Mmm.

I picture a lot of jerks at my funeral, should my body be found, eyes bulging—perhaps only identifiable through dental records. Awful floral tributes with Interflora blooms spelling SON. I can hear the embarrassing sermon by a Benedictine who taught me nothing. My real existence would be glossed over. No mention of Ray. How nice it would be to attend my clone's funeral and watch that mother of mine cry tears for the son she never knew.

I left the buck-toothed creature licking his warm brown lollipop and passed another group of bulky silhouettes among black branches. So many of London's married men, there, doing it. Groaning, groining. Grunting. Full of discontent, disease and despair. Willy waving sour cocks as buggers buggered, while coppers took down the number plates of expensive vehicles in the car park—many containing locked in dogs waiting for their masters to finish their business in the bushes.

Chancing my bike to the bushes, I ran to the pond where Ray and I used to feed the ducks. He'd taken some photos there one time. Over-exposed, only the very blackest parts of my face had shown. Pupils, nostrils, hair, jaw line and the gap between lips.

I flung myself into the deep, inky pond where fish had stopped living. The foul water reeked and the sludge at the bottom felt gross. Still erect, I perched myself on a log to jerk off. The cum I ejaculated no doubt became part of some food chain.

I felt very thin and pale and blurry as I stood by my bike, waiting for more rain. I had a second wank just to keep warm and have something to do.

Unplugging the phone calmed me, I felt instantly lighter. The consequences of my actions were creeping up, internal consequences rattling under my skin. I was beginning to feel increasingly nervy. Twitched out.

I've never had a problem with my Yamaha, or had to refer to the trouble shooting page in the owner's guide but that day there was no sound and I couldn't work out why. It took me an hour to realise that the master volume was on zero. I was pissed off about it but glad that I'd managed to work it out by myself.

Arriving at a LO TOM which I slowed right down, pressing SUSTAIN I started playing simple root chords using the slap bass sound. I saw that my fingertips were extremely white and realised I was fingering with excessive force which could have damaged the terminals. Abandoning any idea of making a recording, I switched off the power supply then plugged the phone back in which was an odd thing to do as it was bedtime. The phone started ringing as the plug entered the socket.

I considered unplugging again. Just for a moment I hesitated. I couldn't resist lifting up the receiver. There were no words, just long-distance crackle and grit, then the line went dead. Pip.

In raised capitals, gold on creamy yellow, one word:

Always

D

If it hadn't been me it would have been someone else. He needed a point of focus. Not many young men would have bought the man a cup of tea unless paid by the hour.

He didn't need *me*, he needed *something* to make up for the long years of loneliness, the difficulty of being a silent queer. Pre '67 was one thing, the disco '70s another. One of the bravest things he'd ever done was place a dumb ad in *The Pink Paper*.

I really should have given him the number of some escort agency.

Friendship cards are both big business and a pain in the arse. Drawn to do a spot of market research, I entered Paperchase purposefully.

Graphic: A bridge. Wording outside: *Cross Over The Bridge To Me*. Wording inside: *Be Mine*.

Graphic: A love heart. Wording outside: *I LOVE YOU*... written maybe twenty times. Wording inside: ...*And The Amazing Thing Is We've Just Met!*

Graphic: Infantile smiley face. Wording outside: *Thinking of You.* Wording inside: *Puts a Smile On My Face!*

Graphic: Clouds. Wording outside: *YOU,* written in creamy yellow on palest blue. Wording inside: *You Are A Part Of Everything I Do...*

Graphic: A lacey pillow case. Wording outside: *Even When We're Apart...*Wording inside: *I Sleep With You In My Heart...*

Graphic: Two words in four different font styles. Wording outside: *I Care.* Wording inside: *I'm Always There...*

Graphic: Flames. Wording outside: *HELL...* Wording inside: *O!*

And there were many, many more, waiting to be signed, sealed and delivered. I felt decidedly light-headed in there, watching the punters making up their minds.

The long-distance crackle and grit went on for longer than usual. It sounded so much clearer than the many answerphone recordings. I could hear him breathing like a bull. A child was audible way off in the distance, screaming. Little birds, too. I'd been expecting the call and nine o'clock on a Sunday morning was his chosen time.

After years of immobilisation, stunned by romantic obsession, wanting but not getting, he was angry. I imagined him as an adolescent, using fantasy and compulsive masturbation as fun, then as a distraction, then to avoid feelings or as a reward or just a time filler for boredom.

"I gave you my number. You could've called me. I think you should've called. Don't you?" Each clipped syllable had the clarity of threat. Here was yet another specimen illustrating the diversity of gay life.

"You're out a lot, aren't you lad? I've spent a fortune listening to your answerphone message."

A countdown had been begun with the arrival of the 'Living Card' he'd sent weeks back. I'd reached ten.

10 "I bet you've been out dipping your wick, haven't you lad?"

9 "Bet you've been slagging your arse up and down Old Compton Street, or in some sauna."

8 "You slag. You gay slag."

7 "I'm a decent, respectable, good, clean-living man and you're not interested."

6 "You know what you are...and you should probably note this down..."

5 You're nothing but a hopeless, heartless little whore."

4 A shaggable, shaggable little tart, whore, queer."

A remarkably accurate description, if delivered in a somewhat melodramatic tone. Nicely put, though, I thought, noting down the definition as suggested.

3 "You bastard!"

2 "You fucking deceiver you."

1 "I'll have your guts for garters!" he peaked.

0 "I only wanted us to be friends."

My telephone manner became very Chinese take-away, saying as little as possible with an emphasis on good manners.

"Tell me..."(Pause) "is there any history of..." (Slightest pause) "...insanity in your family?"

His little breathing irregularity increased.

"Now there's no need to get nasty," he whined.

After a little difficulty with both gripping the handset and the formation of a word beginning with 'y' he managed to blurt: "Y-You little whore!"

I found his pronunciation interesting, delivered like 'who-were'. In the silence that followed I imagined him with a probation teacher's dick in his mouth, then a gun, then both—shooting.

"What do you reckon Joe Orton was reincarnated as?" I asked, perhaps like a BBC2 game-show host.

"A little gay slag like you I should think," he retorted with admirable speed. I felt somewhat honoured and maybe he could tell by my breathing that I was smiling.

"Believe me," he said in the tone of an American Bible-touting huckster, "I'll have you, you young bugger!"

"Yes. I heard. 'Guts for garters,' I think you said. I must fax that to Jean Paul Gaultier."

He slammed the phone down.

Ten minutes later the phone rang, perhaps for a full sixty seconds. I ignored it.

Twenty minutes later the phone rang four times, then stopped.

Thirty minutes later the phone rang twice. Dead silence.

Forty five minutes later, just a little tring to say: *Thinking Of You.*

Shaun nodded quite agreeably when he heard I wanted a number four crop.

"But," he said, "you're certain you want it bleached and dyed orange?"

"Bright orange. That kind of Ziggy Stardust sort of reddish orange," I said. "Like Annie Lennox when she was in the Eurythmics. Rent boy orange."

"Exactement," he shrugged, somewhat resigned to creating this hair-don't. Customer's-always-right attitude.

"I want to look like a hopeless, heartless whore. A shaggable little tart," I said in a whisper with a smile.

"You probably will luv, pale as a ghost with it. Right, I'll just get you washed."

The buzz of the clippers demolished any boyishness left in me. Ten minutes after the bleach had begun to sting, it was rinsed off. When the colour was applied it was like my head had been switched on. Ghastly. Just the ticket.

I thought it must be him with that first prolonged ring of the doorbell. When the letter-box flap started banging I was convinced. With the fist hammering, then the kicking, there was no question about it. This was not the Interflora man.

I crept out of bed ever so quietly to have a peep through the spyhole.

There he was, standing opposite me on the twenty-eighth of August, on the day of his fortieth birthday. He had lacked warmth for so long that he'd opted for hatred to even the score. Having exploded my life through the small ads, the fallout was about to hit.

D-Day.

The view I had of him through the spyhole was extremely wide angled, appropriately distorted. He was red in the face, sweating in his macintosh on what had turned out to be another boiling hot day.

I had known this would happen. Maybe he'd known it would come to this as well. I silently closed the spyhole cover, thankful that it was of the kind that avoided the giveaway sign of lightening/darkening in the tiny lens. I returned to my bed, curled up under the duvet and waited for the racket to stop. What I heard was Jessie telling him to piss off.

I crept around the flat all morning, keeping away from the windows. Every once in a while I tiptoed into the hallway to check that he wasn't still on the doorstep outside. It was the strangest feeling when I came face to face with him through the spyhole hours later, to find him staring directly into it, listening out for signs of life inside.

It was when I went to the toilet that my guard slipped. If I'd looked at the letter-box I would have seen that it was raised and that his two black, shiny eyes were peeping in, catching a waist down glimpse of me in nothing but a pair of old Calvins taking a leak.

Taking another peek, certain he'd have moved himself along by that time, I got quite a shock when his hand thrust through the letter-box and grabbed the waistband of my briefs. He'd rammed fist and forearm in, grazing both. Veins in the hand quickly swelled up from the grip of the letter-box, tiny drops of blood staining my pants and skin. Each one of his fingers held fast. He just wouldn't let go. His shouting turned to high pitched, repetitive screaming.

"You *are* a whore. I *know* you are are whore!"

I had to rip the pants off to avoid them tearing into my scrotum and up the crack of my arse. Once off, they were dragged backwards through the letter-box. Maybe he was thinking he'd actually ripped them off me.

It was Jessie who phoned the police. When the ringing of the bell and banging of the letter-box flap started again, interrupting the six o'clock news, I strode the lightest of steps into the hallway. Through the spyhole I came face to face with a man in white shirt-sleeves and a black and white peaked cap. I could see Dai standing there, looking silly. I could see Jessie framed in her doorway wearing an apron.

I opened the door. All three blanched at the sight of me. It wasn't the Boy George teeshirt they were looking at, nor the baggy cut-down Levi's with huge buckled belt or unlaced DMs. It was the hair-don't.

Tears streaked his face. A clear mucus slimed his upper lip. The staircase stank of him.

"You look ridiculous," he whined.

Jessie went back inside and shut her door but I bet she got busy behind her spyhole within seconds.

"Have you come about the drains?" I inquired.

"There have been complaints," the officer said, nonplussed.

"I'm sure there have. Be a sweetheart and pop the old fool off at King's Cross before he misses the last train."

I couldn't have been camper.

I turned on my heel as the officer was getting his notebook out. The doorbell rang once. I put on the new Felix single at maximum volume, returning to watch the officer have a few harsh words with Dai, tucking his notebook into his back pocket. Then they both left.

Through carefully adjusted venetian blinds I saw Dai hail a cab. The armpit of his macintosh was many shades darker than the rest of his raincoat. Inside his tightly packed cells a gene spelled N-U-T-T-E-R.

I put the kettle on.

Those fine, resourceful folk in Hamamatsu have provided customers with fifteen demonstration songs in the depths of the machine's circuitry. I'd never had the inclination to hear the delights stored within the SONG SELECT section before, but I was in a mood to try something new.

Unplugging the headphones, I listened to a few bars of Edelweiss (09) through the internal speaker system. Then, using the OUT jack to deliver the pathetic output through my stereo—close to maximum volume—I treated anyone walking along the Goswell Road to four classics chosen at random: *Carmen* (04), *Happy Birthday To You* (20), *House Of The Rising Sun* (08) and *Greensleeves* (13).

I wished for rain, heavy rain, the kind I like best, to wash scum off the streets, down into the drains. The forecast said everything was going to be just fine. I felt like getting beautifully drunk. I briefly considered phoning Glenda. I ended up having an early night.

The letter-box flap was up. Being invisible had put me in a new, elusive rank. Where was I? What was I up to? What had become of what's-his-name? Invitations and press releases had begun to dribble through once again. There was no mail. Nothing.

I unlocked and swung the door open. No one there.

I bent down to look through the letter-box to see the view Dai had stolen of me. I checked around the hallway in case some correspondence had nose-dived and skidded somewhere. Nothing.

Dai had been, that's what I thought. Back. Back to get me. I was more inconvenienced than scared. I wanted to be anonymous, uncontactable and untouchable. I wasn't.

Neither was my letter-box, letting in piss-stinking air from the staircase.

Feeling the way I was feeling, nothing, I could quite happily have slashed my wrists. Slashed my wrists, or jumped off the balcony. Perhaps slashing my wrists as I fell from the balcony, my blood wetting me in a sudden, heavy shower like the rain I like best.

I've always liked the Sex Pistols' cover of Iggy's *No Fun* as much as the Stooges' original. Ideally there'd be two mixes available, featuring the vocal talents of Lydon and Pop over the two different backings. One time I lined up Pistols on CD, Stooges on turntable, to make a rough mix. Didn't work, but I had a lot of fun trying. It was one of the last things that gave Ray a good laugh.

I was feeling like going out to a place of wild, natural beauty, getting my cock severely sucked or getting my head kicked in. Funny. Not funny. What I wanted most was to be an orphan. I wanted to disappear, without anyone worrying blandly about me.

It was one of those days when I'd decided to have the phone plugged in. Living dangerously. Picking up the receiver to ask, "Friend or foe?" brought silence.

"It's your mother," the woman who'd borne me announced, with as little enthusiasm as Ray had delivered the words when we were together. "How've you been?" she asked, only wanting to hear good news.

"Fine," I said, slipping into another voice. "Busy."

"What have you been up to?"

"Oh, things you could never imagine."

"You don't know what I could imagine."

It was a strange thing for my mother to say. There was a pause, which was quite exciting. Excitement is rather rare when it comes to conversing with any member of my family. I wondered if Dai had been on the phone to her.

"Oh Liam," she said, voice rising, sounding like her mother's. "Come home, Liam. It's your Dad. I tried phoning before but there was no answer."

"What's up?"

There was a pause in which I crossed my fingers.

"Your father passed away, eleven o'clock this morning."

My reflection was warping so nicely in the kettle, shaking the crossed fingers loose. Christmas had come early. I had to turn away from the warped semi-circle of teeth, the corners of my mouth folded up, so as not to laugh out loud.

"I'm sorry, Liam," my mother said, as if she were in some way responsible for disrupting my social life over the next few days.

"How did he go?" I asked.

Through sobs:

"He hit one of his moods after walking the dog. I could hear him coughing in the toilet. Then I heard him fall. The doctor says it was a heart attack."

Just like Elvis.

I called a cab then phoned the operator to say I wanted to change my telephone number. By the time I'd confirmed this in writing and packed a bag, the driver was knocking at the door. Within a minute of being in the cab I decided on a detour to Soho. Shaun was going to have to do something about my hair.

After years of hoping and private planning, he'd died—just like that. I was robbed of two particular pleasures: the cruel, hard gaze I'd direct at him from the foot of his bed while he experienced—point two—a short but painful exit.

The fact that he'd finally kicked the bucket would be a turning point for my mother and release her from those *splitting* headaches.

My father's funeral left a lot to be desired. Everyone was there, the majority drycleaned especially for the event. The weather had turned cold, September was feeling like February. I wore a grand, jet-black Saville Row coat my father hadn't got much wear out of. The Paul Smith suit Ray had deviously acquired, but never worn, fitted well. Black.

I was told in a number of Irish accents what a good man that father of mine had been. It seemed a fair idea to just nod a little and keep my mouth shut. Women had put their heads under hair-driers, men had dressed slowly, applying eye-watering drenchings of aftershave, probably thinking of the business of the will. It seemed like every Irish couple in need of a sandwich and Guinness from Greenford, Hanwell, Kentish Town, Camden Town and Ealing had turned out, equipped with one clean handkerchief which was shared. I didn't know a lot of the people there. That was a comfort.

Outside Ealing Abbey, Church of St. Benedict, I studied the flick-up and root perm of the woman from the prefabs in Hanwell as her beefy legs struggled up each of the sixteen steps. My mother had rescued her in the Parish Centre one night when she was ruining her make-up, diluting gin with tears. A peroxided woman who ran up bridal ensembles from Pronuptia patterns on a machine in her kitchen, working round the clock through a haze of nicotine and appetite suppressants to cater for the bad taste needs of the local community. Mrs Piana. What a woman.

Tawny, dusky pink base foundation was favoured by all the aunts, one even wearing it on the back of her hands to hide liver spots. Ray always took great pleasure in tearing a strip off the relatives, outdrinking the men, pushing the boundaries of a dirty joke with the women, teaching the children rude words and inappropriate hand movements they'd grow into.

The top-of-the-range coffin was carried by six serious men, not unsurprisingly in black and white, only worth mentioning as it looked so out of place on those chaps who'd surely all once served as car park attendants.

As a prepubescent I'd served on this altar. I enjoyed giving the incense a mean swing, ringing the bell like a go-go boy in slow-motion.

Along that same aisle my parents had trotted to marry. Along that same aisle all four innocents had been marched for Baptism, First Holy Communion, then meaningless Confirmation. Along that same aisle sculptured flounce affairs in masses of moire with iridescent pearl motifs, pie crust edgings, wired chiffonette bows shot with silver, dozens of silk roses (blooming and also in bud), teardrop pearls on necklines, lace sashes and rococo themes on veils had drifted. Cunningly concealing foetuses beneath all that swirling silver satin and ivy leaves; packs of cigarettes and emergency make-up in heart-shaped pockets; tattooed forearms under trailing sleeves of antique effect lace in economic polyester.

I was glad it was a funeral and not a wedding. I've always found the spectacle of so many poorly matching hats hellish. Not having to move on to a reception with a display of vibrating electric blankets, digital egg-timers, hostess hotplates and the obligatory wok all neatly ticked off the pressie list was a relief. Black was kinder to people with so little colour sense.

The opening chords of a hymn I didn't recognise sounded up. The organist, however, was familiar: a useless retired music teacher who used to drone on about the joys of camping by the sea.

I put one arm around my mother as she hyperventilated

discreetly, placing my dry face on show as I stared back from the front row to witness the advance of the coffin—breaking with all rules of etiquette of course, absorbing clouds of poisoned darts shooting my way from Irish eyes which weren't smiling. I wondered if his jaw had fallen open in death the way it did in front of the telly so often. Perhaps it had been superglued shut. Eyes too.

The paid for solemnity of the march down the aisle was upstaged by a cousin's "special" daughter, Tara, who got busy tearing pages out of a holiday brochure she'd dragged through her life for the past four years. She shouted, "I want go Malta!" God made us all different and he made little Tara very different.

The idea of selling ices, soft drinks and popcorn crossed my mind when my mother was hamming up her dutiful mourning widow performance.

I'd only been to one funeral before. Ray's. The funeral he'd prepared for himself was particularly riveting. No chance of reggae at this send-off. Or OutRage! teeshirts. In death, Ray became not the stink I last saw, but a kind of pure essence of himself, a knot of happy memories defying chronological order.

Since my father's death I've been seeing things his way a little. I probably caused him a few (hundred) disappointments. Personally, I don't give a fuck.

I wasn't nervous but hungover from days of watching my mother go through cupboards and drawers, wiping out all trace of that man's existence. I got through quite a few bottles of QC Sherry prior to the big day. People said I was taking it real bad, looking so pale. Gaunt. "Ah yes, he'll be missed." "Such a loss." My arse. I was celebrating, delivered from evil at last.

I felt nothing for the panto around me as the priest spoke of the monster who'd impregnated an egg in my mother's womb with a couple of splashes, passing on those genes. I was more than ready for another sherry and a slice of Soreen by the end of the service.

The pace of the drive to the graveyard was painfully slow.

The Lord is my shepherd, I shall not want,
He makes me lie down in green pastures,
He leads me beside still waters,
He restores my soul.

Watching the falling of soil in that Southall graveyard was frustrating. My memories required a much greater depth of burial. There were far too many people about for me to spit discreetly down into the old grave.

Why can't life be pink and fluffy? Like a picture book. Why can't life be soft and sweet?

Once the dirt had been pushed over him, six feet down, all cars sped away.

I kissed my mother on the cheek and sneaked out the back-door when everyone was too pissed to notice, not staying on to empty the ashtrays or hoover up. I was tired of being a son. I was tired of being alive.

It was strange travelling by London Underground after so long on the bike. Didn't seem as bad as I remembered.

The Edge is one of those Soho faggot watering holes which goes to town pretending to be laid back in a New Age kind of way. Lots of varnished wood, stainless steel and lighting you wouldn't notice. Very Key West. A colour scheme suited to a multi-ethnic reception class. Upstairs it's all very meeting room, show flat. The downstairs area is split into two sections, a below deck ambience bar and a long narrow cafe effort on the street. It's a hip place to waste time. When people get hungry they go to the Hare Krishna restaurant next door.

It was shortly after four. A group dressed in boots, beads and huge buckled belts stood in ballet positions by the stairs, chewing what I guessed to be sugarfree gum. Cash-corrupted fools, waiting to be toyed with and tortured, singing along with another remix of Donna Summer's *I Feel Love* and meaning every word of it. Doomed but beautiful wretches, waiting to be wined, dined and sixty-nined.

My eyes fell on the open back pages of *Boyz*, pages neatly spread as if ready for me. Like a hint, like an arrow saying, This way.

Sling, stocks, toys, red, duos.
Dungeon, playroom. SW17.
Uniform, CP, Bondage, games.
Hotel visits. Brian, 0181 682 —— /
0956 ——. C Cards.
e-mail: Brian.esc@msn.com

God bless Brian. And Fabrizio the XXVWE Latino,
every stinking inch of construction worker Toby, along with
Derek (22) in Victoria—5 mins from tube (Recent photo)
and the new, genuine ex-soldier Steve. Fit, tough, versatile
manly good looks, 6` 2``, Can do duos—the lot! Aiden, BJ,
Jesus and Jock. More than just the one Mr Gay UK
contestant, the occasional porno star and poet. God bless
them all, every last queer lad, and there are pages of them
winking anyone and everyone their way from thirteen quid
a week picture boxes. Just waiting for your call. Picture
boxes in *Boyz*, *Thud* and *QX* where little is left to the
imagination as to what their best physical asset might be.
  Call me. No, call *me*. Hey, I can be over in ten
minutes…just pick up that phone.
  A detonation of laughter. The lights dimmed a bit.
Music up.
  The barboy who served me had flesh and blood encased
with skin still tanned from weeks on a beach all by himself.
Ivory fingernails, perfect smile, prepared for compliments. A
handsome, fiercely groomed, gym-trained young man with
no whiff of 'the game' as yet. Security ✪✪ Sex ✪✪✪✪✪
Style ✪✪✪✪. This wearer of one jumbo sized silver hairgrip
sing-songed the inevitable *Can I get you something?*
  I fancied a fruit juice (I'd been tipsy for days), but when
he cocked his lovely ear to my mouth I asked for a whisky, a
double. I had the feeling he was fresh to London, learning the
ropes. I wondered what he'd be like a month on, having
danced the nights away at GAY, Queer Nation, Fruit, Fridge,
Heaven, Trade and The Beautiful Bend, places where sweat
drips off noses, pours off walls, runs in rivulets down the
small of backs to make arse-licking salty. He was very handsome, innocent. An attractive target to conquer. (How long

CALL ME

170

before the straitjacket of gay identity suffocated him?) Despite that giant hairgrip he was still not quite yet a fully paid up narcotic narcissus. (How would he look if he ever reached the ripe old age of thirty?) I wondered if prostitution would be entered into with the planning, calculation and premeditation a farmer devotes to fields of maize. Or a contact ad fanatic choosing and reviewing sex. Sex as an experiment, a game with changing rules. A commodity. A very special need.

This way.

An anonymous sexual compulsive in search of a fresh face, a new body—some magical quality to feel complete—fixed his sad eyes on me in hopeful anticipation, sitting up and leaning just a little forward like a stuck up, bitter and twisted judge about to pass sentence. So I fixed my eyes on dancing queens braving the change of weather in JPG kilts on Soho Square, drinking from bottles in brown paper bags, wearing teeshirts which would be trashed by October after a lovely little shopathon. Daggy pop-tarts who pay so much attention to their smells, stars, scars and choice of Scotch in bars. So busy all of a sudden with their mobiles. Topic of conversation: a fab bit of e-mail? The latest T.4 cell count? Surely, no surely not Ms Kylie Minogue. Place your bets.

The state of anticipation this particular sexual compulsive was trapped in was exhausting him. He'd perfected that wanna-lick-yer-arse-this-minute look with years of practice, flashing across his forehead more garishly than the pulsing neon of Roppongi. This way.

As Madonna finished singing a song which compared her to a virgin being touched for the very first time—for the ten millionth time—the old fool put on his glasses gingerly, changing from the pair of reading glasses he'd scoured *Boyz* with. He wanted a jolly good look at that blur swamped in black. To him I was just the sum of my body parts and the whiff of a memory. Gay love is not blind. He would have recoiled at the sight of a concave chest, double chin or absence of copious bulge in the ding-a-ling department. It wasn't my CV he wanted to get his hands on. He wanted prime, pumped, waxed, tanned, moisturised boy-flesh. No short-dicked man. He stared, gobbling up the curves of the nasty piece of work who'd quite happily buried his father just an hour back. I turned the pages of *Boyz* so he'd see I'd deliberately diverted my eyes.

ON THE JOB

GAY SEX HOT ACTION WITH MEN AT WORK

010 592 596 ***
DOCTOR's EXAMINATION
Spanked on the cheeks by the company medic

010 592 596 ***
BANK MANAGER's MEETING
Steve takes it all for a loan

010 592 596 ***
POLICEMAN's BEAT
Caught with his pants down in the cottage

010 592 596 ***
BUTCHER's BOY
Bent over and pumped on the block

010 592 596 ***
PERSONAL TRAINER
Black muscle man gets pumped and rammed

010 592 596 ***
FISHERMAN's FRIEND
Sticking his 9" up his catch

010 592 596 ***
JOURNALIST's INTERVIEW
Probed by his dick

010 592 596 ***
BUILDER's SITE
Rough builders slide their fingers up him

010 592 596 ***
TOILET ATTENDANT
Peephole view of the city boys sucking hard

010 592 596 ***
LAWYER LUST
Barristers pull their briefs down in the loos
Calls charged at 84p/min cheap rate and £1.04 at all other times.
Calls terminate in Guyana.
Sexplay Services, PO BOX 2745, London E1

Calls terminate in Guyana? It always pays to read the small print.

I looked out of the window as a gang of Hare Krishna devotees bounced by, banging drums and singing something easy enough to learn the words to. I wondered if there was a pattern to the man's absenteeism at work. Wondered what he'd say to me in a mirrored room with fifty nine minutes to go.

When I turned around he was still staring, teacup in hand, like I was the creature he'd been waiting all his life for. I prayed he'd soon be hovering up and down Queer Street, off to Crews, Brief Encounter, Halfway to Heaven or Kudos…stumbling the noisy jungle/desert of the Metropolis, sitting inside the vacancy of his hopes…or raking through those exciting imported magazines in the basement of Clone Zone. Maybe he'd have felt more at home on a massage table at Earl's Court Clinique, No 9 or Image in that yellow rubber jock-strap he'd treated himself to not half an hour before in Regulation…or on the stained bedsheets of any number of musclebound little darlings available in the free papers all in the name of a bit of fun he couldn't quite explain. The tired-out boot-licking, piss-drinking, finger-frigging, tit-tweaking, love-biting, arse-licking, shit-stabbing, mother-fucking, spunk-loving, ball-busting, cock-sucking, fist-fucking, lip-smacking, thirst-quenching, cool-living, ever-giving useless man.

But what did I go and do? Only flash him my 'Ooh, I could make you feel so good' look.

And when the corners of his mouth began to curl up in a horrible smile, I leaned forward to whisper,

"It'll cost you."

A-Z
UNDERSTANDING
THE TERMS

KEY WORDS AND ADVERTISING VOCABULARY ABBREVIATIONS

Many of the words and phrases are as you'd expect...

WLTM: would like to meet

36 yo: age can be stated using yo (years old), or numerically.

5` 11``: this refers to height.

8``: an entry in inches usually refers to supposed length of erect penis.

seeking 25-35: desired age range sought after.

1-2-1: supposedly seeking a sincere, one to one relationship.

501s: a range of Levi's jeans.

NE: North East, geographical areas are often specified.

Some are a little more obscure...

A: active.

abs: abdominal muscles.

Accu-Jac: male masturbation device, an electrically operated vacuum pump connected to a sleeve which fits over the penis, providing a gently sucking movement. A 'buddy' attachment allows usage by two males simultaneously. Accu-Jac II is also equipped with dildos for anal or vaginal insertion.

AC/DC: bisexual.

accident prone: interest in urination, often when clothed. See WS/water sports.

AIDS: Acquired Immune Deficiency Syndrome.

ALA: all letters answered.

ALAWP: all letters answered with photo.

Amyl Nitrate: heart drug, often used to enhance dance and sexual experience.

any: anywhere. eg London/any.

A/P: active/passive.

apricot: chubby chaser

AT: animal training. (Submissive partner is treated as a dog or some other animal.)

auto-fellatio: capable of providing themselves with oral sex.

AYOR: At your own risk, advice sometimes offered in gay guides in connection with cruising areas such as parks.

BD: bondage.

B&D: bondage and discipline.

BND: boy next door.

B no D: bondage, no discipline.

beefcake: masculine/muscular.

beige: rimming.

Bike: popular brand of jock strap, also Bauer and Black.

BJ: blow job.

Bk: black. (Eyes or hair.)

Bl/Bl: refers to eye colour (blue), hair colour (blond).

black: heavy S&M/whipping.

black & white: hanky worn on left indicates a liking for black bottoms, worn on the right to indicate a desire for black tops.

blow: (blow job) fellatio. Can also refer to drugs.

blue: Can indicate 9" or over; interest in bruising.

bona: Polari for fabulous. (Also title of short-lived gay television guide in the UK, 1994).

boots: interest in footwear, boots in particular.

bottom: passive partner in anal intercourse/S&M.

bottom man: passive partner in anal intercourse/S&M.

boxer shorts, boxers: Interest in boxer shorts, underwear.

Br: brown. (Eyes or hair.)

Brd: beard, bearded.

brogues: interest in City gent type footwear.

brown: interest in faeces.

buns: buttocks.

butch: masculine appearance and/or behaviour.

buttplug: sex toy, artificial penis.

C/B: cock and balls. (Penis and testicles.)

C/BT: torture of cock and balls. (Torture of penis and testicles.)

C Cards: credit cards, occasionally seen in ads for masseurs and escorts.

chaps: Western style clothing which covers the legs but leaves the crotch and rear on view. Popular in S&M circles.

cheese: waxy accumulation under unwashed foreskin.

chicken: underage male.

chubby chaser: homosexual seeking obese male.

cln shvn: clean shaven.

clone: New York Village/San Francisco variety of 70s gay with exaggerated macho appearance & behaviour.

closet, in the: homosexual not admitting sexual orientation.

cock ring: pubic ring used to strengthen erection, enhance orgasm.

cock tease: someone who acts as though s/he wants sex but has no intention of following through with the act.

combats: interest in uniforms.

come: semen.

contract: agreement between those engaged in S&M activities. Often a safe codeword is used.

CP: corporal punishment, spanking.

CS: clean shaven.

cut: circumcised.

cut-offs: shorts made by cutting

longer leg covering garments, usually jeans.

D: divorced. (Occasionally used for Dominant.)

denim: interest in Levi's, Lee, Wrangler, Edwin, Big John Jeans

dick: penis.

dildo: sex toy, artificial penis.

DIY: masturbation. Nothing to do with putting up shelves.

DMs: Dr Marten's footwear, boots favoured by skinheads and labourers. Became a major fashion item in the early 1980s.

drag, in: dressed up as opposite sex. Also Polari for clothes.

EC: European Community, used in Mixed sections of contact ads where a person is seeking (a marriage partner) of the opposite sex. See MBA.

endowment: male genitalia.

equipment: male genitalia.

EWE: extremely well endowed.

firm hand: corporal punishment interests, spanking.

fist fuck (FF): penetration of anus with fist.

FFA: penetration of anus with fist and forearm.

frank letter: a request for graphic descriptions, nude photo.

French: fellatio.

French dressing: ejaculate of semen into mouth during fellatio.

fruit: gay male.

fuschia: spanking.

G: gay.

gayper: free gay paper such as *All Points North, Boyz, Gay Community News, Guyz, The Pink Paper, QX, Thud.*

generous: often implies that the person is willing to pay for sex.

GL: good looking.

glory hole: hole cut in toilet wall to look through, exchange notes, fellate, penetrate.

goatee: a style of beard.

gold: interest in threesomes.

Greek: anal intercourse.

green: indicates money. Used by a sex worker or someone willing to pay for a sexual service.

grey: bondage. (This might also suggest Discipline.)

GSOH: good sense of humour.

GWM: gay white male.

H: can mean hot, hairy, humpy, husky, handsome, hung.

hand job: masturbation.

handball: penetration of anus with fist and forearm.

HIV+: body positive. Person infected by the virus which can go on to cause AIDS, (Acquired Immune Deficiency Syndrome).

hz: hazel. (Eyes.)

J: Jewish.

jack off (J/O): masturbation.

JO: jack/jerk off.

JPG: Jean Paul Gaultier.

jock strap (J/S): support for genitalia. Item of clothing for athletics/posing.

KY: water based lubricant used for anal intercourse.

L: leather, also Latin.

LDU: leather, denim and uniform.

length, a bit of: Penis.

limits respected: agreement between S&M participants, often with safe codeword.

L/L: leather/Levi's.

load: unejaculated semen.

loaded gun: penis before ejaculation.

love muscle: penis.

lunch: penis.

lunch box: male genitalia.

magenta: interest in armpits.

M: married. Also, male. In S&M context, masochist or master.

Mary: gay male. (Effeminate).

master: dominant partner in sado-masochistic sex.

mauve: naval fetish.

MBA: mutually beneficial arrangement, often a marriage to gain legal status.

navy blue: large penis, nine inches or over. (See Stryker, Jeff.) May indicate a liking for bruising.

nephew: young male, often sought after by an older man for a small fee/presents.

no fees: will not pay for services rendered.

no J/O: no jacking off (not interested in letters from people who receive sexual gratification from letters/phone conversations, without meeting up).

no Pros: not interested in hearing from male prostitutes.

NS, N/S: non smoker.

NSP: non smoker preferred.

NSPBNE: non smoker preferred but not essential.

no strings: contact without commitment.

NTL: no time limit. A term used by sex workers.

no timewasters: advertisers who are (supposedly) conducting a sincere search tend to use this. It asks people to reply only if meeting the criteria, as a deterrent against voyeurs, practical jokers and prickteasers.

No. 1/2/3/4: cropped hair, No. 1 being close to shaven.

nuts: testicles.

O: oral, (fellatio.) Also, orgasm.

OHAC: own home and car.

olive: military interests.

orange: prepared to do anything, anytime—supposedly.

OTK: over the knee, an interest in CP.

out: openly homosexual lifestyle.

OutRage!: London based queer rights direct action group.

P: passive.

PA: photo appreciated.

packet: male genitalia.

paisley: interest in boxer shorts.

pecs: pectoral muscles.

pierced: body piercings, most commonly found on ears, nipples, eyebrow, scrotum and penis. And labia.

pink: colour most frequently associated with gay life after gays were forced to wear pink triangles under Nazi regime. [*Hanky code*, pink: dildo interest; dark pink: tit torture.]

pistol: penis.

playroom: S&M oriented room invariably equipped with a sling, restraints and tools to administer pain.

plug, to: anal intercourse.

POC: person of colour.

Polari: gay slang.

popcorn: rhyming slang for horn, erect penis.

poppers: Amyl or Butyl Nitrate.

P/P: photo/phone.

prefect: the passive partner in corporal punishment (CP) scenarios; however, sometimes a prefect can administer.

pricktease: someone who acts as though s/he wants sex but has no intention of following through with the act.

purple: piercing interest.

QX: free gay weekly paper.

Rd: red hair.

red: interest in fist fucking.

Dark red: double fisting.

rent, rent boy: male prostitute.

R/F: rear French. Oral-anal contact.

RN: Royal Navy

rim, to: to lick/suck anus.

rough trade: working class/coarse/dangerous male, often heterosexual but permitting some sexual acts such as fellatio.

S: can mean slave or sadist. (Context is obviously important.)

SA, S/A: straight acting.

sado-masochism, (S&M): leather interests, includes domination, degradation, pain.

safe sex/safer sex: sexual activities that avoid transmission of bodily fluids to prevent sexually transmitted diseases eg, kissing, masturbation, body rubbing, or use of condom for penetrative sex.

scat: faeces.

scene: gay scene or sex scenario.

schoolmaster: dominant partner in corporal punishment scenarios, spanking.

scumbag: condom. Derogatory expression suggesting depravity.

shaving interests: interest in shaved bodies, removal of body hair—possibly scalp, too.

shoot, to: to ejaculate.

sixty nine: mutual fellatio.

size queen: gay attracted by penis size.

skin: skinhead.

skinflicks: gay porno films/videos —also the name of an explicit American magazine.

slut: promiscuous gay male.

S&M: sado-masochism.

smegma: interest in waxy build-up under unwashed foreskin.

smoke: invariably marijuana, rather than cigarettes.

snuff movie: pornographic film in which sexual excitement is linked intimately with torture and final murder of the star/victim.

SOH: sense of humour. (Helpful if cast in a snuff movie.)

Speedo: a brand of swimwear, interest in. Other makes are Arena and Head.

SPOC: seeking person of colour.

stiffy: erect penis.

Stryker, Jeff: porn superstar of the late twentieth century. (See Navy blue.)

straight: heterosexual.

straight-acting: not flamboyant or obviously gay.

T: torture.

TBH: Polari for to be had, desirable.

teddy bear: interested in touching, cuddling.

Teletext: a UK television service. Page 394 features contact ads.

tits: pectoral muscles/nipples, in relation to men.

TLC: tender loving care.

toilet: interest in urine, possibly faeces.

tool: penis.

top man: active partner in anal intercourse.

toys: sex aids, implements, tools. (Dildo, nipple clamps, whips, chains etc.)

trade: non-gay male, often a manual labourer. Permits some sexual acts.

training: sports variety or, more usually, activities for slaves to endure.

TS: transsexual.

TT: tit torture.

TV: transvestite.

uncle: older man, invariably seeking a nephew.

uncut (U/cut, U/C): uncircumcised.

Uniforms: interest in uniforms.

vanilla: sex without fetishism, cuddling etc.

verbal: verbal abuse/humiliation interests.

versatile: gay who performs a

181

variety of sexual acts.

VGL: very good-looking.

videos: interest in pornographic videos.

VWE: very well endowed. Large penis.

W: white.

wad: unejaculated semen.

water sports (WS): interest in drinking, giving, getting soaked in urine.

wax: interest in pouring melting wax on to naked flesh. A common form of S&M play.

WE: well endowed. Large penis.

white: interest in masturbation, usually mutual masturbation.

WS: water sports.

XL: extra large. Usually refers to length of penis when erect. Not always to be believed.

XWE: extra well endowed.

yellow: interest in urine. Pale yellow: spit.

Y-fronts: interest in underwear. Popular brands: Fruit Of The Loom, BVD, Calvin Klein, Jockey and Hom.

P-P Hartnett grew up in West London. His photography has been featured in *The Sunday Times*, *ES magazine*, *The Face*, *The Independent*, and *Time Out*, and exhibited in New York, Tokyo and London. He has also worked as a teacher of children with special needs. He is currently at work on a second novel and a book of short stories tentatively titled *I Want to Fuck You*.